Liza's Avenger™ by Erin
Copyright © 2015 by Erir
ISBN: 978-1518899584
Published by Flagship Fic
Publishing™

GW00792550

Copyright © 2015 Command Group International LLC

Denver, Colorado, United States of America

Cover art and design by Mary C. Findley (https://www.pinterest.com/marycfindley/all-about-book-covers/)

Map art and design by Robert Altbauer (www.fantasy-map.net)

www.flagshipfiction.wordpress.com

Liza's Avenger

Erin Burnett

To my sister Ailsa, thank you for all the support and cakes

Praise for Liza's Avenger *by Erin Burnett*

"Great first effort by a young but talented storyteller looking to inspire a new generation of children with a message of hope and salvation. At times, Liza's Avenger reminded me of my own childhood memories of The Wizard of Oz, The Legend of Zelda, and Chronicles of Narnia, to name but a few... If this is the quality of work Erin Burnett can produce before she's even ventured beyond her teenage years, I'm excited to see what wisdom, university literature experience, and polish will do to enhance her obvious talent in years to come. I have a feeling we will look back one day and say, 'this is where it all started.' "

- Nicholas Downing, Author of Talon's Test and the Shield of Faith

"For a first full novel by a Northern Irish young woman, Liza's Avenger is a very good book... you quickly become involved with the story, and it's a good one even though the plot is very familiar. The characters are almost entirely very young and have personalities to match. However, their character is far better than average. The world building is sufficient and consistent. So, I can easily recommend this for your pre-teens and teenagers. It's a clean, fun read."

- David Bergsland, Author of Daniel's Mighty Men

Prologue

"Do you understand what is expected of you?"

Five individuals were sat around a table, their attention turned to the youngest member as they awaited his answer. The room was dim and elongated shadows obscured their faces.

"You are certain we need a human child to complete the experiment?" he answered, unsure.

"Yes," replied their leader. "Is that a problem?"

"Surely children are innocent..."

"There is no such thing as an innocent human. Would you prefer to continue to live under their oppression as we have done for decades, too afraid to show your face for fear of being slaughtered merely because of your identity?"

"No, sir," he replied meekly. "I will do what you ask of me."

"Where will we get it from?" somebody else asked.

"Not a city. There will be too many people. They could overpower us in our current condition. Target a village," the leader replied.

The youngest member arose from his seat to carry out his task. He felt deeply uneasy, but when he thought of the alternatives he felt he had no choice.

He would kidnap a child.

Chapter 1

Hikari poked the wood in the stove, trying to get it to burn. She wasn't very good at cooking, but ever since her parents died she'd had no choice. She grinned as the stove finally lit. Now she just needed some food.

There was already a bowl of apples sitting on the table her younger sister picked that morning. Her sister Eliza was six years old, and everyone in the village of Honif called her Liza. Despite being sisters, Liza looked nothing like Hikari. Liza's hair was blonde and long, but Hikari was a brunette and her hair was only shoulder length. Hikari was also a lot taller than Liza, as there were ten years between them. Their only similarity was both girls had the same shade of blue eyes their mother had. Since she was thirteen, Hikari had been raising Liza. Even after three years, she still hadn't learnt how to properly cook.

I sent Liza out to get food from the storage room half an hour ago, thought Hikari. *What's taking her so long?*

Hikari left her house and went to look for Liza. Honif was a very small village, with only five people living there. It was a stretch to even call it a village. Hidden away in the trees, the village rested in a small clearing of the Honif forest in a secluded and peaceful part of the Maysea Continent. Residing in Honif were Hikari and Liza, Mr and Mrs Firr, a middle-aged couple who grew food in a small patch of land outside their house, and Anlon, the Firr's seventeen year old son.

Mr Firr was out sowing seeds. He waved at Hikari as she passed by. He was a well-built middle aged man with slightly tanned skin from spending most of his time outdoors. He stood in stark contrast to his wife, who was lean and pale.

"Is Liza still in the storage room?" Hikari asked as she waved back.

"Yes," Mr Firr paused to laugh. "She mentioned something about forcing you to eat broccoli."

"I'd rather eat dirt," replied Hikari, and Mr Firr laughed again.

"You two sure are something," he said. "Remember, Florence and I are always there for you."

Hikari smiled.

"I know. We appreciate all you do for us."

In the months after their parents' death, Hikari and Liza were completely dependent on the Firrs. They fed them, made their clothes and tried to educate them as best as they could. Hikari had now taken over the tasks of cooking and teaching Liza to read and write, but Mrs Firr still made their clothes. Hikari had tried learning how to sew in the past, but the needle went through her finger more than the cloth she was trying to sew. She hoped one day she could repay the Firrs for all they had done for her.

Anlon Firr also helped the village. He stood at the entrance to Honif forest and stopped any monsters from getting into the village. He was tall, lean and had scruffy blonde hair. Occasionally he would try to flirt with Hikari, but she never took him too seriously. She believed the only reason he showed interest in her was because she was the only girl he knew around his age.

He had a sword he forged himself and was forever showing off about it. Anlon's dream was to leave Honif and have some sort of adventure. Hikari had left the village with her father a few times to buy supplies, but she had no desire to go adventuring now. She liked her life the way it was; peaceful and surrounded by people who cared for her.

Monsters were quite rare around Honif, but there were a few. They were an unwelcome reminder of the by-gone magic era, when humans became reckless with forbidden powers and created vicious animal hybrids which soon bred out of control. Magic was now banned throughout the continent after many wars had been waged over it. As the generations went on, the breeds of monsters became weaker and weaker. They were a minor threat.

Hikari made her way to the storage room. It was a small, dimly lit underground room where all produce was stored in various barrels and crates. Liza was standing on her tiptoes and picking bits of broccoli out of a barrel.

"Liza!" Hikari yelled as she pretended to be cross. "What have I told you about forcing me to eat broccoli?"

This startled Liza, who hadn't noticed Hikari coming into the storage room. She squealed and fell backwards onto the floor.

"Serves you right," said Hikari as she pulled Liza back up on her feet.

"You're such a meanie!" exclaimed Liza as she gathered up the food she had dropped. "You're having EXTRA broccoli tonight."

Hikari groaned.

That stuff is possessed. All evil and green...

Liza grabbed Hikari's hand and dragged her out of the storage room.

"You will eat what I tell you to eat," huffed Liza as she pulled Hikari towards their house.

Anlon laughed as he watched the sisters bicker.

"Remind me which one of you is the eldest?"

"Go back to playing with your sword, Anlon," Hikari snapped as Liza continued to drag her.

They went inside their small, single roomed house. The furniture was very simple, most of it having been made by their father who was a skilled carpenter. The only imported item was a large wood burning stove which used to be the pride of their mother. Hikari tipped the vegetables Liza gathered into a pot of water she had collected from the stream and left it to boil on the stove. She also added in a small amount of beef that had been imported from a nearby kingdom.

One of the benefits of living in Honif was you didn't have to pay taxes to a ruler. However, the downside of being independent was everything you couldn't make or grow yourself had to be imported. Honif's only source of income was from selling produce from the Firr's farm, so they could only afford a small amount of beef.

Hikari stood by the pot daydreaming of a time when Liza was only three and her parents were still alive. Her mother could always cook amazing dishes, even with the simplest of ingredients. They were a lot better than the watery stews Hikari made. However, Liza never complained. She ate whatever Hikari gave her. Hikari wished she could be like her, but she would never, as long as she lived, eat a piece of broccoli without complaining.

Hikari snapped out of her daydream when she heard Liza yelling at her.

"Hikari! The pot is boiling over!"

"Oh snap..." muttered Hikari as she salvaged the stew from the violently bubbling pot. She divided it into two clay bowls and placed them on the table.

"Sorry for the slight taste of burnt."

As usual, Liza ate the stew despite its less than appetising appearance. She then stood over Hikari and forced her to eat every last bite of hers. When they were finished the sisters tidied away all the pots and bowls and Hikari put Liza to bed. She started to read her a book her father wrote when he was still alive. It was a simple story and Hikari read it to Liza nearly every night. It was about two sisters.

In the story the younger sister was always causing trouble for the older one, but they still loved each other regardless. The story ended when the older sister became old enough to leave the village. She walked off into the sunset, promising to return to the younger sister. The ending always made Liza cry, and every night she would make Hikari promise if she ever left Honif she would come back to her. Liza also insisted on praying each night, a practice Hikari had long since abandoned. Their parents had been devout followers of an ancient religion called Christianity, a belief system which emphasised a personal relationship with God. It supposedly originated from a far-off land named 'Earth'. According to the legend, the people of Earth had technology far more advanced than that of Maysea and were able to reach the people of Maysea using vessels which could only be described as flying ships that could sail across the stars.

Hikari had no time for what she thought were nothing but nonsensical fairy tales for children. However, Liza was comforted by the prayers, so Hikari did not try to stop her. After all, evening prayers was one of the only memories Liza had of their parents. As she opened her eyes to sneak a peek at Liza, Hikari was forced to admit her sister's appearance during prayers was almost angelic as she knelt by the side of the bed with her hands clasped together, earnestly praying. Eventually, Liza fell asleep and Hikari put the book back on the shelf.

I wish everyday could be like this... Even with the burnt broccoli stew. I hope Liza grows up to be the person our parents wanted her to be.

Hikari blew out all the candles around the house and lay down next to Liza.

"Sleep tight."

***

Hikari awoke to another peaceful summer day in Honif. She was out helping Mr Firr harvest some crops, and Liza was in the storage room sorting the produce into the correct barrels.

Thank goodness last night's stew used up all the broccoli... Hikari thought as she planted new crops. It was hard work, and dirt got under her fingernails as she covered the onion bulbs with soil.

Mr Firr stopped to wipe the sweat from his brow.

"I think Florence had some herbs she needed planting," he said as he resumed ploughing the ground.

"I'll go and get them."

Hikari ran over to the Firr's house and let herself in. It was a house similar to the one she and Liza lived in, but it was slightly more spacious and the windowsills were decorated with flowers of various kinds. Florence Firr smiled at Hikari as she came in. Florence was a kind woman who had been like a substitute mother for the two sisters. Her brown hair was flecked with a few grey hairs.

"Mr Firr sent me to get some herbs," Hikari explained.

Florence put down the garment she was mending (a shirt Anlon had torn) and went to reach for some plants growing on the shelf above her head.

"Sure thing, love. They're over here..."

She was abruptly cut off by a loud explosion that rocked the house and sent the herbs toppling onto the

~ 12 ~

ground, their pots shattering upon impact. The blast was so powerful the ground shook and several books fell from a shelf on the wall.

"What was that?" Hikari yelled.

A cold panic went through Hikari's body as she made her way outside, Florence following nervously behind her. The scent of smoke immediately hit her, making her eyes water and her nose burn. She almost gagged.

A large crater had been made where the farm used to be and a young man was standing in the centre of it. At least, he appeared to be a young man. At first glance Hikari thought the stranger was human, but when she looked closer she noticed his hair was an unnatural shade of red and he seemed to be floating a few inches off the ground. He closed his eyes and held his hands out in front of him. A strange ball of energy was formed and he fired it into the village. Each ball made the ground shake upon impact. Anlon was struggling to stop the man, but he was extremely overpowered. Mr Firr was desperately trying to defend himself with a hoe.

Hikari looked around in shock. The destruction had happened in a matter of seconds.

Hikari remembered hearing legends when she was very little about a tribe of humanoids called Kellua who had the ability to float. The only things that distinguished them from humans were their vibrant hair colours and a distinctive teardrop shaped mark under their left eye. Kelluas were also said to be incredibly skilled in magical combat. According to the legends Hikari had been told, the entire Kellua tribe had been destroyed in a war against humans hundreds of years ago.

Why? What is a Kellua doing in our village? What does he want?

Liza's still in the storage room! Hikari realised in horror. She grabbed the hoe she was using earlier and ran towards the storage room. *Please be safe, Liza!*

Hikari had no idea what the Kellua wanted or why he had targeted Honif, as there was nothing of real value in the village. All she cared about was keeping Liza safe.

Hikari found Liza in the storage room. However, she wasn't the only one there. Hikari's heart lurched as she saw another Kellua standing in front of Liza. The male Kellua was wearing a long cloak which reached past his knees, the same shade of blue as his hair. He didn't look much older than Hikari.

"You are perfect for our experiment. Please come, and I will not hurt you," said the Kellua. He reached out his hand.

"No!" screamed Liza. "You're a monster!"

The Kellua sighed and shook his head.

"Must I take you by force? It's really not my style. I prefer negotiating. But if needs must, I suppose I have no choice in the matter. The Superior will not accept failure."

The male Kellua raised his hand and an eerie blue light encompassed it. Hikari opened her mouth to scream at him to stop, but she was too late. The Kellua cast the blue light towards Liza, who was knocked off her feet and for a second her entire body shone with the blue light. She then collapsed onto the ground.

"Oh dear. It seems I used too much power. I often forget how fragile human children are."

Hikari was horrified. She prepared to run at the Kellua using her hoe as a weapon. He flinched, as he was not keen on fighting.

"You monster!" screamed Hikari as she ran at him.

Hikari dodged the blue orbs the Kellua was firing at her and she hit him repeatedly with the hoe. She wasn't normally skilled in combat, but seeing Liza on the floor had sparked something inside of her. She had never been so angry, and all she could think about was attacking her sister's assailant.

"Strong one, aren't you?" he muttered as he failed to dodge Hikari's blows.

The Kellua was panting now and she could tell he was wounded. He took one last look at Hikari before running out of the storage room as fast as he could. Hikari let him escape. She had a far more pressing concern to worry about now.

Liza lay on the ground, unmoving.

"Liza..." Hikari's voice was nothing but a hoarse whisper. She fought back tears as she held Liza in her arms.

Hikari hugged Liza daily. Her sister's tiny body had never felt so frail in her arms. She was reminded of the moment she held Liza for the very first time after she was born. She had been terrified she would break her.

Liza opened her eyes. Hikari knew Liza must have been in a lot of pain, but despite her discomfort she smiled up at Hikari.

"You'll be ok, Liza," Hikari promised. "I'll make you better. I'll take you to a kingdom with the best doctor in the world."

Hikari desperately tried to reassure Liza, but even as she spoke she knew she was losing her. Hikari got the feeling she was trying to reassure herself more than Liza.

"I'm tired, Hikari..." mumbled Liza as her eyes began to close. "Can we talk in the morning?"

"No," Hikari was pleading with all her heart. "Don't go to sleep. Keep talking to me."

"I love you, Hikari."

Liza's ragged breath stopped.

"No..." Hikari whispered. "NO!"

Hikari set Liza's body back on the ground and started to cry, violently. Her world had been shattered.

Mother, Father... and now Liza. Must everyone I love leave me?

Hikari slammed the ground with her fist and collapsed in tears. She couldn't believe Liza was dead; she was expecting to wake up and discover it was all a nightmare. She repeatedly slammed her fist on the ground, trying to wake herself up. Her hand began to bleed. Mindlessly, Hikari watched the crimson blood trickle on to the ground.

***

In a dreamlike state, Hikari surveyed the damage. Honif was gone. What used to be houses were now piles of burnt rubble. The farm was reduced to a burnt hole in the ground. Black smoke rose up from the rubble, some of it still smouldering. On the ground lay the tattered remains of her father's book.

Hikari buried the dead. She made gravestones with what materials she had. She used pieces of wood which had once been part of her house and used a stone to carve in the names of the dead. She placed the few flowers she could find on the four graves. It started to rain, but Hikari didn't care. She didn't care about anything.

Anything except revenge.

The rain fell in torrents, erasing the ink from the book. The picture of the smaller sister waving at her older sister as she left the village was carried off by the rain.

I will avenge Liza. I will destroy the Kellua who did this. I will destroy anything that gets in my way.

With that mission set in her heart, Hikari left Honif without looking back. Honif, her birthplace and the only home she'd ever known, was now nothing more than a dark and dreary dream.

Chapter 2

Hikari made her way through the Honif forest, fuelled by her rage. She pushed her grief to the back of her mind and let herself be consumed by her hatred for Liza's killer. She swiftly dealt with any monsters who dared to cross her path.

There was a small beaten path connecting Honif to another town called Dunin. Dunin was a large farming town, and Hikari had visited it many times with her father to get supplies for the village. She hadn't visited in years, but as she first glimpsed the town between the trees she realised not much had changed.

The town consisted of a group of small wooden houses surrounded by fields filled with crops and livestock, and a river to the east. The town also had an inn and a small weaponry shop, although Hikari had never been inside them before. She decided she would need a new weapon, as a hoe wasn't exactly the most deadly weapon in the world.

The only change she noticed in Dunin was the hut on the other side of the river. It must have been built since Hikari's last visit, as she didn't remember it being there before.

Hikari composed herself before entering the town. She couldn't afford to let emotions interfere with her mission.

First I'll ask around and see if anyone has seen a Kellua.

She wiped the tears off her face and approached a burly man working in one of the fields.

"Excuse me sir, have you seen a blue or red haired Kellua recently?"

The man laughed at her question.

"You actually believe in those old legends? Even if such creatures did exist, we wiped them all out years ago. Someone's been telling you tall tales, missy."

Hikari resisted the urge to bring her hoe down on the man's head.

"If you don't believe me, go north through the Honif forest. You will see the remains of a ruined village. A Kellua destroyed it."

The man continued to laugh.

"Who would bother attacking there? Why don't you go back home like a good little girl, or make yourself useful and give me a hand here? "

Hikari walked off in disgust. She asked more people but received similar answers each time. No-one in the town believed the Kellua tribe still existed.

Hikari was in a foul mood and she was even more furious when she visited the weapon shop and discovered the small amount of money she was carrying wasn't enough to buy anything, even a simple slingshot.

She was on the verge of leaving the town when she remembered she hadn't yet sought out whoever was living in the hut across the river. A local woman noticed Hikari looking at the hut.

"That's Kerry's house."

"Kerry?" Hikari couldn't recall meeting someone called Kerry before.

"Yes, she's only lived here for around a year. I'd be wary of visiting her. She's a little... strange. Always leaving the town for days on end. No-one has any idea where she goes."

If this Kerry person is always going in and out of Dunin, she might have seen the Kellua who attacked Honif. She's my last hope in this town.

"Is she at home now?" Hikari asked the woman.

"I believe she is, yes."

"Great, thank you," Hikari said as she smiled for the first time since entering the village. She crossed to the other side of the river using some precariously placed stepping stones.

I'm probably getting my hopes up over nothing.

She knocked on the door.

She heard a crash and the sound of footsteps coming from inside the house. The door flung open, revealing a girl who was around the same age as Hikari. She had long hair that was a shade of light purple, and she was wearing an expensive looking knee-length dress. At first Hikari feared she was another Kellua, but she lacked the facial mark.

Her hair, the way she dresses... She looks very out of place in a small farming town.

"A VISITOR!" she squealed. Kerry grabbed Hikari by the wrist and dragged her into the hut before shoving her into a chair.

"No-one EVER visits me!!"

Hikari could see why. A foul odour filled the air and all the furniture was scratched. There were cats everywhere; under chairs, on top of the bed... There was even a cat sitting on top of a shelf. How it got up there was anyone's guess. Hikari felt uncomfortable as countless pairs of feline eyes were directed her way.

"I'm Kerry! What's your name?"

"Hikari."

"Hika-WHAT? I think I'll just call you Snappytaps."

Where did this girl come from? Crazycatland?

Hikari was about to ask Kerry about the Kellua, but Kerry continued to talk before Hikari could get a word in edgeways.

"So, Snappytaps. Why do you look so sad? Smile!"

"If you must know, my parents died in an epidemic years ago. This morning, two Kelluas destroyed my village and killed my six year old sister." Hikari replied, rather coldly. It pained her to say it, but she knew she would have to face what happened head-on if she was ever going to get on with this conversation and get back to seeking justice for Liza.

For a second Kerry was shocked, but a wide grin soon returned to her face.

"Ooh, bummer. Cheer up, it could be worse."

Again Hikari felt the familiar feeling of wanting to hit someone.

"How could it possibly be worse?"

Finally, Hikari shook her head. Arguing with Kerry was going to get her nowhere.

"Look Kerry, I came here to ask if you have seen a Kellua lately."

"A Kellua? You mean those weird floaty aliens from the legends with crazy-coloured hair and they look sort of like humans?"

"Yes."

Kerry thought for a moment.

"Well, the other day I was taking my cats for a midnight walk through the forest..."

Taking cats for midnight walks? I'm not even going to ask.

"And when I was on my way back home I saw these guys with funny hair running through the forest. They looked pretty irked."

"Really?" Hikari shouted as she jumped to her feet. "Where did he go?"

"Enthusiasm! That's how I like it! Much better than being depressed!"

Hikari surprised herself by laughing. Kerry's optimism was infectious.

"Shut up and tell me where he went."

"How can I shut up AND tell you where he went?" asked Kerry as she folded her arms.

"Now listen here, I have a hoe and I'm not afraid to use it," joked Hikari as she pointed her hoe at Kerry's head.

"A hoe? You want to fight a Kellua with a hoe? Are you crazy, Snappytaps?"

Geez, she's calling ME crazy?

"I fought him with this hoe before, but he got away. I need to find him if I am to avenge my sister."

Hikari wasn't laughing anymore. Her optimism abruptly faded as she was reminded of her mission.

"He was heading south. Are you sure you want to go after him? It really isn't smart to fight an irked Kellua," Kerry said, with concern in her voice.

"I'm sure. Thanks for the information, Kerry."

Hikari headed for the door.

"Uh... Hikari?" Kerry asked hesitantly. "Could I maybe... you know... come with you?"

Somehow, I knew she was going to ask that.

"I don't know. If you come with me, what about all these cats?"

"Oh, the cats aren't mine. They're strays I picked up on my way to this town. I'm sure they'll be fine. Please can I come with you? Pretty please?"

Kerry looked at Hikari with pleading eyes.

She reminds me of Liza, on the night before her birthday. No matter how much she would plead, I'd never let her see her presents. Perhaps that's why I've taken to Kerry. She reminds me of Liza.

Travelling with her couldn't hurt. She seems to know a thing or two about the local area. And besides, both of us could do with a friend.

"Fine. You can come. As long as you don't get in my way."

Kerry grinned.

"But first, I'm dragging you to the weapon shop. The hoe has to go."

Kerry grabbed Hikari's wrist again and dragged her out of her house, across the river and into the weapon shop.

"Do you mind not dragging me everywhere? I can walk on my own, thanks."

The shopkeeper looked shocked and slightly worried as Kerry entered the weapon shop and started browsing the displays. Kerry wasn't the sort of person you would trust with a dangerous weapon.

For a small shop the choice was extensive, from pocket slingshots to bow and arrow sets so large the girls could barely lift them. For herself, Kerry selected a long sword out of a display rack. The silver blade glinted beneath the light, and the leather hilt was encrusted with various jewels. For Hikari she picked something more unique. It was a weapon that resembled a scythe, with a long decorative shaft topped with a long, curved blade.

"Is this the best you have?" Kerry asked the shopkeeper.

The shopkeeper nodded.

"They're 500 Raha each."

Hikari gulped. *That's 1000 Raha! I'm only carrying 5 Raha. How on Maysea can we afford these?*

Kerry detached a leather bag that had been hanging off her belt. She tipped the contents onto the shopkeeper's table with a clatter. Hikari and the shopkeeper both gasped. They had never seen so much money in their lives.

Kerry started to count out the amount they needed to buy the weapons.

"340... 450...500....750...800...950... There! 1000 Raha!"

She pushed a pile of coins towards the shopkeeper and put the rest back in the bag.

"We'll be taking these!"

Kerry lifted the weapons and handed one to Hikari.

"Hey, shopkeeper. You can keep this hoe," said Kerry as she threw Hikari's hoe on the ground. The shopkeeper was too shocked by what had happened to object.

Hikari and Kerry walked out of the shop.

"So what now? We walk south in hopes of finding these Kellua dudes?" Kerry asked as she reattached her moneybag onto her belt.

"I know we don't have a lot of information to go on, but this island isn't very big. The only town we have left to ask around in is Port Gorm."

Hikari had never been to Port Gorm, but she knew it was a port at the very south of the island that was the only way to reach the mainland. It was the town where Mr Firr used to go to export produce from the Honif farm.

"There's also a ruined castle between here and the port. It hasn't been occupied in hundreds of years; it would be a good place for someone to hide," Kerry suggested.

Kerry sure is full of surprises. She knows everything there is to know about this island, and she's extremely rich. What is she doing living on her own in a small house with nothing but a bunch of stray cats to keep her company?

Hikari decided not to ask any questions. Kerry was being very kind to her, despite having only met her. Her back story was none of Hikari's business.

Together they left Dunin. The weather was perfect for travelling, and the two girls walked at a fast pace across the flat plains. They hoped to reach the castle before it got dark. The idea of searching an abandoned castle in the middle of the night did not appeal to Hikari. Kerry led the way, with Hikari taking up the rear. The journey was mostly uneventful, apart from encounters with a few weak monsters and Kerry managing to get both feet stuck in a swamp. After about three hours they could see the castle in the distance. The weapons they bought in Dunin were excellent for slaying monsters, but the downside of them was they were very heavy and as a result, Kerry's pace quickly began to slow.

"Can we rest, please?" begged Kerry, who looked like she was ready to collapse.

"Fine," replied Hikari, who was in need of a rest herself.

Hikari sat on a rock and shared a water canteen Kerry had brought.

"I'm sorry if I'm offending you or anything, but is that your real hair colour?" Hikari asked, looking at Kerry's strangely coloured purple hair.

"Nah," Kerry replied as she ran her hands through her hair, "I dyed it with this weird purple fruit I found on the mainland. I think it looks awesome."

"It's certainly interesting," Hikari said, with a bemused look on her face.

Kerry got up on her feet.

"Come on, let's go and test out these new weapons on a certain Kellua."

She grinned and started to run in the direction of the castle, which was visible in the distance.

"Hey, wait!" cried Hikari as she picked up her stuff and chased after Kerry.

It wasn't long before they reached the castle. It was a tall building made of stone that was nearly hidden by ivy growing all over the castle, suggesting no-one had lived there for many years. The castle boasted one turret that was mostly collapsed into ruin. It was a sorry sight. The bravado of the girls faded slightly as they looked at the castle.

Nervously, they walked through the crumbling entrance arch. The interior of the castle wasn't much different from the outside. There was no furniture, just stone walls covered in ivy and the remnants of a carpet clinging to the floor. A spiral staircase led up to the next floor.

"Let's check out upstairs. Don't make a noise, if he is up there we want the element of surprise to be on our side when we attack him," whispered Hikari.

Kerry nodded and she crept up the stairs behind Hikari. Hikari tried to calm herself so her anxious breaths would not give them away. When they reached the top of the stairs they were startled to see two male Kellua who appeared to be arguing with each other. Hikari instantly recognised one of the two as the Kellua who killed Liza, the other was the one that attacked the village. His red hair stuck out at various angles and he was wearing a similar cloak to his accomplice. He looked like he was in his 20s, assuming Kelluas aged the same as humans.

Hikari dragged Kerry behind a wall, where they quietly eavesdropped. Hikari's heartbeat was so loud she was surprised the Kellua couldn't hear it.

"Face it Kyros, you failed. Not only did you fail to bring me what the master requires for his experiment, you also left a witness alive. What if this child spreads word that some of our tribe are still alive? What if the humans unite and rise against us and history repeats itself? And this time it would be only five Kelluas against all the humans!" said the red haired Kellua in a stern and condescending voice.

The blue haired Kellua, Kyros, hung his head in shame.

"I realise that, Michius, but the survivor... She was something else."

Michius, the red haired Kellua, laughed.

"Defeated by a human. A female human child, no less. Saya would love to hear about this."

"We'll find another child somewhere else. Next time, I promise I won't let you and the Superior down," said Kyros, with a hint of desperation in his voice.

Hikari saw something move in the corner of her eye. To her astonishment, Kerry was calmly walking towards Kyros and Michius.

"Hey! What are you guys talking about?" she said with a carefree attitude.

"Kerry, what are you doing?" hissed Hikari.

Is she trying to get us killed?

Michius spun round. A look of fury and hatred filled his eyes when he saw Hikari and Kerry.

"HUMANS?" he spat.

"It's her!" screamed Kyros in genuine terror. "She's the survivor from Honif!"

Without delay, Hikari and Kerry drew their weapons. Michius and Kyros elevated themselves a few centimetres off the ground and started shooting orbs of blue and red energy at the girls. Kerry ran at Michius, and Hikari aimed her attacks at Kyros. They clumsily dodged the orbs as they were thrown, some of them narrowly missing contact by a hair.

"This is for what you did to my sister!" Hikari cried.

Hikari landed an attack on Kyros' arm at the same time Kerry hit Michius on his leg. Michius cried out in pain and sent an orb of red energy in Kerry's direction. It hit Kerry in the chest and she was knocked off her feet.

"Kerry!"

Michius used Hikari's distress as an opportunity to send her flying. For a moment Hikari and Kerry lay on the floor stunned, but they were soon back up on their feet.

"Change of strategy!" yelled Hikari as she dodged an orb of energy. "We both go for Kyros first!"

Kerry nodded and both girls raised their weapons and charged towards Kyros.

Hikari remembered from the legends that Kelluas did not bleed when injured, but a blow to the head could knock them out cold, or even kill them. That was the point of their floating ability; it was supposed to stop their attackers from being able to render them unconscious. Hikari was very grateful her parents had taken an interest in mythology. She never imagined she would be using what they had told her in bedtime stories as combat techniques.

Kyros wasn't floating, as he was too distracted by the pain Hikari had inflicted by attacking his arm. Both their weapons came down on Kyros' head and he screamed before collapsing on the floor. He wasn't dead, but it would quite some time before he woke up.

Michius saw Kyros sprawled out on the floor and he sighed. He landed on the ground and put his hands in the air as a sign of submission.

"You girls aren't half bad for a couple of kids."

"We're only getting warmed up," said Hikari as she hesitantly lowered her scythe.

Michius picked up Kyros' unconscious body and threw him over his shoulder.

"Next time, I shall defeat you," he sneered before disappearing in a flash of light.

"Hey, wait! Come back here!" yelled Kerry, but the Kellua had already disappeared.

"Since when can Kelluas teleport?" exclaimed Hikari in amazement.

Kerry shrugged her shoulders.

"We didn't avenge your sister."

"No. And from the sounds of things, they're going to target more kids for this 'experiment'. We can't let what happened to Liza happen to anyone else," Hikari said as she clutched her scythe. "Before they knew we were eavesdropping, they said there were five of them. It will be nearly impossible for us to defeat them on our own, but we can try. It's better to die trying than to do nothing at all."

Kerry nodded, impressed by Hikari's resolve.

"We should head to Port Gorm. We've already missed the last sailing to the mainland, but we can stay in the inn overnight and catch the first morning sailing," explained Kerry.

"How come you know so much about this island, Kerry?" Hikari asked.

Kerry hesitated for a minute.

"I've been travelling," she said, while avoiding looking Hikari in the eye.

A silence filled the air, a first for Kerry. Hikari eventually broke it.

"Anyway, I agree. Let's get to Port Gorm before nightfall."

Kerry smiled, her excitement restored.

"Yeah, let's do it."

***

Somewhere far away, a female Kellua with long pink hair was sitting by Kyros' bedside.

"Beaten by a bunch of girls... I'll never let you live this down."

Michius shook his head.

"At least wait until he's conscious before you start tormenting him, Saya."

"You too, Michius. I bet the Superior was thrilled when you reported back," Saya sneered.

"Obviously, he wasn't happy with us. But what could I have done? Continue fighting while Kyros was knocked out on the floor?"

"Stop placing the blame on Kyros. You're both hopeless. I can't wait until the Superior lets me get my hands on those little human pipsqueaks," Saya laughed and cracked her knuckles.

"Do you think the Superior is right? I admit I have my doubts about his plans," Michius wondered out loud.

"To be honest, I don't think the Superior really knows what he's doing. But at least we're actually doing something after all these years of hiding out in caves, secluding ourselves from the world we used to own," muttered Saya as she fixed her hair into a ponytail.

"I hope the Superior's recklessness doesn't lead us to our deaths," Michius muttered.

Chapter 3

Hikari and Kerry reached Port Gorm as it was getting dark. It was an interesting town. All the houses were built on stilts which stuck out of the water, and a series of wooden walkways connected the houses. The smell of fish in the air mingled with the salty scent of the sea. Fishing was Port Gorm's main industry. The town was busy with people returning home after a day's work.

Hikari had never seen the sea before, and she stared at it in amazement. The shining blue water stretched as far as the eye could see. As a girl brought up in a very small environment, she found its vastness mind-boggling. The setting sun added to the scene as it slowly sank below the horizon.

"Amazing, isn't it?" said Kerry when she saw the look of awe on Hikari's face.

They made their way to the small inn. Like all the other buildings, it was a wooden house on stilts. They ate some freshly caught fish before settling down for the night. It was the first time Hikari had ever eaten fish. Hikari knew from now on she would be experiencing a lot of firsts.

Kerry fell asleep immediately, but Hikari lay gazing up at the ceiling.

Has it only been 24 hours since I was reading to Liza before she went to sleep? Tears rolled down Hikari's face when she thought of Liza. *That was the final time I'll ever read to her.*

Hikari fell asleep with the tears still falling.

Morning came, and Hikari and Kerry went to the docks to get a boat to the mainland. On their way there they were approached by a girl who lived in Port Gorm.

She looked about ten years old. Her hair was plaited and she wore a simple cotton dress.

"Are you travellers?" she asked excitedly, her grin revealing several large gaps in her teeth.

"Yeah, we're on our way to the docks," replied Kerry, smiling at the girl.

"You should look out for the lost princess!" she said enthusiastically.

"Lost princess?" asked Hikari with interest.

"Yeah! People have been saying a princess from one of the mainland kingdoms has been missing for over a year. If you find her, her parents are offering a HUGE reward! I want to try and find her, but I have to stay on this island."

"That's interesting. Can you tell us more about her?" Hikari asked.

The girl was about to reply, but Kerry grabbed Hikari's wrist and dragged her towards the port. Hikari shook her wrist free.

"What was that for?" Hikari shouted at Kerry. "If we got the money for finding the princess, I wouldn't have to depend on you to buy me everything!"

"What if the princess had a reason for running away? What if she doesn't want to return home? Did you think of that?" Kerry snapped.

This was the first time Hikari had seen Kerry angry over anything.

"OK, sorry. Let's get to the docks."

They arrived at the docks and waited for a ship. The waterfront was crowded with all sorts of ships setting out for the day, from small fishing boats to large cargo ships.

"Sorry Snappytaps," said Kerry apologetically. "I shouldn't have lost it."

"It's OK," smiled Hikari. "I guess I'll have to keep on relying on you to buy me everything."

"I don't mind," replied Kerry. "I couldn't let you walk around with nothing but an old hoe."

A large ship sailed into the docks. Immediately many dock-workers jumped on board and started unloading various crates filled with cargo. Other dock workers were busy loading on crates filled with local goods.

A young man who was carrying the last crate onto the ship turned to an older dock worker.

"Is this it? I thought there was another farming village that shipped out produce."

The old man shrugged his shoulders.

"There should be a few crates from Honif, but I guess their farm mustn't be doing well this season."

It looks like news of Honif's destruction hasn't reached the rest of the island yet. It's not like many people bother going all the way up there. It will probably be a while before people realise what happened.

"Passengers may begin boarding! Pay upon boarding! Stowaways will not be tolerated!" yelled a burly looking man from the deck of the ship.

Hikari and Kerry walked up the gangplank and Kerry gave the man at the top a handful of coins. The deck of the ship was mostly covered in crates, with a few wooden benches for passengers. The ship was fairly quiet, with only a few other passengers.

"Have you ever been on a ship before, Snappytaps?" asked Kerry as she sat on one of the benches.

"I've never gone further than Dunin. How do these things float? They're so big!" Hikari remarked in amazement.

"To be honest, I don't know how they float. But they do, and that's what matters. It should only take about four hours to reach the mainland on a calm day like this," said Kerry.

The crew ran to the side of the ship and hoisted the anchor out of the water. They then sat at the sides of the ship and started to row. Hikari watched them, fascinated by the whole process. At first she found the motion of the ship sickening, but she soon got used to it.

"If it was windier they would use a sail," said Kerry, pointing at a massive rolled up piece of material on top of the ship's mast.

Kerry soon fell asleep, and Hikari sat on a bench gazing out at the sea. The island got smaller and smaller as they got further away.

I wonder if I'll ever return to the island.

Hikari felt sad to leave the place where she was born and raised, but at the same time she could barely control her excitement at going to a new land. She promised herself she would return one day when she had destroyed the Kelluas.

After a few hours, the mainland could be faintly made out on the horizon. Hikari shook Kerry awake.

"We're almost there!" she said with a grin on her face.

Kerry stretched and rubbed her eyes.

"It's been a while since I was last on the mainland," she yawned.

"Are we anywhere near your hometown?" asked Hikari. She wanted to see what kind of place Kerry came from, to see if it really was a crazy cat land.

"My hometown? No, that's very far away. Very, very far away. The town we're going to dock at is a huge city called Alana. It's so big; the castle is literally about the same size as Dunin."

"There's a castle? Do you think that's where the princess went missing from?" Hikari asked.

"Yeah, I think so. The ground floor of the castle is a massive library that's open to the public," said Kerry. "We should check it out; there could be books on the Kellua tribe."

"Sounds like a plan."

The Alana docks slowly came into view. Countless ships lined the docks, loaded with all sorts of foreign goods. Beyond the docks was the city, and like Kerry said, it was huge. Hikari was speechless at the sight of all the smooth stone buildings shining in the midday sun. The streets were paved with stone, and horse-drawn carriages ran through them. The only sign of plant life were the flowerboxes in front of several of the buildings, which were filled with colourful blossoms.

The ship's crew lowered the anchor and Hikari and Kerry jumped off the ship. To Hikari's surprise, Kerry pulled the hood of her dress up over her head, concealing most of her face.

Surely she's not cold! It's roasting out here!

"You lead the way," said Hikari.

Kerry led Hikari through Alana's streets, often stopping to give Hikari time to gaze at something she'd never seen before. Most spectacular was the huge fountain in the town square. It was a marble statue depicting angels playing trumpets, with jets of water falling into a small pool below from the bell of the trumpets. Another thing which fascinated Hikari was a small ice cream stall on the side of one of the streets, and she spent all of her 5 Raha buying a strawberry flavoured ice cream that she nearly dropped when she tasted it and was shocked at how cold it was.

"What did you expect from something called ice cream? Emphasis on the word 'ice', Snappytaps," laughed Kerry.

"Quit calling me Snappytaps!" yelled Hikari between licks of her ice cream.

"How do you expect me to pronounce Hik…Hikki… Whatever your name is…."

"It's no worse than Kerry," said Hikari. "Anyway, you used my name back at the castle. You have no problem pronouncing it."

"Look, one minute you're desperate to keep travelling, and next you're sitting here stalling and eating ice cream."

Hikari quickly finished eating the ice cream cone.

"Fine then, enough stalling. To the library!" shouted Hikari, and she took off down a street.

"Hey, Snappytaps!" yelled Kerry. "The castle is this way!"

Kerry pointed in the opposite direction Hikari was running.

"I think I'll follow you," said Hikari sheepishly as she turned back.

"One little ice cream and you're hyper. Remind me to never let you eat that stuff again," said Kerry.

They walked on towards the castle. A few people shot strange looks at the two teenage girls walking through Alana with huge weapons, but most ignored them.

At last they reached the castle gates. The castle was a huge marble building, with many turrets and a moat surrounding it. A wooden drawbridge crossed the moat. The inside was equally as grand, with tiled floors and silk curtains hanging over pristine windows. It made Hikari feel awkward and out of place as she stood there in filthy travelling clothes.

"The library is over there," said Kerry, pointing at a huge door to the west of the entrance hall. "Go on ahead; I have some things I need to do while I'm here."

She ran off before Hikari could object. Hikari decided to leave Kerry to whatever she was doing, and she walked into the library. Never in her life had she seen so many books. Ginormous wooden bookshelves lined the walls from floor to ceiling, all filled with books. Several desks with chairs were available to read at. The library was fairly quiet, with only a few people in browsing the books.

How am I supposed to find anything in here? If I was to look at all the books, it would take me days! And how am I supposed to get at the books on the shelves above where I can reach?

"Excuse me, ma'am…" said a timid voice from behind Hikari. "Do you need any help?"

Hikari turned round to see the owner of the voice. Standing there was a girl who looked around twelve years old. She had long blonde hair tied up in white ribbons, and she was wearing a black and white dress. Pinned to the top of her dress was a badge saying 'Kamitika – castle librarian' in gold lettering.

"Yes, I was wondering if you have any books on the Kellua tribe," said Hikari, grateful she wasn't going to have to search every shelf.

"Just a moment, I'll check the catalogue," said the librarian.

She ran over to a huge book that was on a desk in the middle of the library. Hikari followed her and watched as Kamitika searched through the book. In the catalogue every book in the library was accounted for. The books were listed alphabetically and, in addition to the title, other details were documented such as 'shelf number' and the last time they were borrowed from the library.

Kamitika flicked through the book skilfully until she found what she was looking for.

"On shelf number five in bookcase number eighteen, there is a book on the ancient war against the Kellua tribe."

Hikari smiled.

"Thank you!" Hikari said to Kamitika, before walking off towards bookcase number 18. Shelf five was filled with books on ancient legends, and Hikari could tell by the amount of dust covering the books that no-one had read them in a while. She found a book entitled 'The legend of the Kellua war', and she pulled it from the shelf and sat down in a chair to read it.

I wish Kerry would hurry up.

There was a small table beside the chair Hikari was sitting on, and the local Alana newspaper was on top of it. She decided to flick through it while she was waiting for Kerry to come back.

There wasn't anything of particular interest to her. A few minor thefts had taken place on Market Street, a tailor had started his new clothes making and mending business on Poppy Street and the price of fish was set to rise due to the falling fish population in the sea surrounding Alana.

Hikari was about to roll up the newspaper and set it back on the table when an appeal on the back page caught her eye. It contained a painting and a description of the missing princess.

She gasped and almost dropped the newspaper.

Her hair was shorter and a different colour, but there was no doubt about it.

The missing princess was Kerry.

Chapter 4

According to the newspaper Kerry had disappeared over a year ago, leaving only a short note scrawled on a piece of paper saying she would never be back.

This explains everything. Why Kerry dyed her hair, why she lived alone in Dunin, why she had so much money and why she covered her face when she got off the boat.

Hikari didn't know what she should do. Should she continue travelling with Kerry and never let on she knew her secret, or confront Kerry about it? She decided she would talk to Kerry and find out why she ran away. Who wouldn't want the life of a princess?

Now I need to find her.

She set the book back in its proper place on the shelf and went to find Kerry. On her way out Kamitika smiled at her and asked if she had enjoyed her time in the library.

"Yes, thank you. I'll come back as soon as I find my friend," Hikari replied.

She walked back into the entrance hall and went towards the door Kerry had gone through. Hikari found herself walking down a set of plain stone stairs.

This must be the servant's area of the castle. What is Kerry doing down here?

She walked down the steps into the kitchen. It was a huge room with many large wood burning stoves and countless pots and utensils. The carcasses of various animals hung from the roof, ready to be cooked.

Kerry was sitting in the corner, playing with two cats.

"I missed you two so much," she said while stoking one cat with each hand. "Have the cooks been feeding you properly?"

"Found you," said Hikari, interrupting Kerry's conversation with the cats. "I found you, Princess Kerry."

Kerry looked at the ground.

"I suppose I have some explaining to do."

* * *

Hikari brought Kerry to the library and they sat down in a corner, away from people who might overhear their conversation. Kerry still had her hood up.

"I'll start from the beginning," said Kerry.

"I'm the second in line to the Alana throne, and my sister Rhianna is first in line. She's eighteen; two years older than me. Growing up, Rhianna was the one everyone fussed over. We were both tutored in many subjects and Rhianna excelled in all her studies while I would be lucky to get a single question right. My parents decided to get me extra tutoring, but I would usually hide in the kitchens and play with the cats. My father was furious with me, and he and my mother spent more and more of their time scolding me and keeping me in line. Rhianna began to resent me for stealing all of our parents' attention, and she refused to speak to me. By the time I turned 15, my parents were at the end of their tether and Rhianna still refused to speak to me. It became obvious to me I would never be what they defined as a 'proper princess', so one night I left. The librarian, Kamitika, helped me escape. She was also the person who dyed my hair for me."

"Are you and Kamitika close?" Hikari asked.

"She's the only person in the castle I could call a friend. When she was little she would always visit the library to look at the books. Her mother was always sick, and she liked bringing books home to read to her. Her father was never around. When Kamitika was ten her mother died and my father agreed to let her live in the servant's area of the castle. She became the official castle librarian. I felt guilty leaving her, but I was tired of causing my family so much pain. So one night I asked her to help me leave without being seen."

This is a lot to take in, thought Hikari.

"How did you escape?"

"Kamitika dyed my hair with some purple fruit from the market and gave me a cloak to cover myself with. She let me out the back entrance that would normally only be used by servants. I then hopped aboard the first ship to the island and I ended up living in Dunin for a year. Then you turned up, and I suppose that's the entire story."

Kerry sighed. Clearly, telling the whole story had taken a lot of effort. Hikari then asked her the question she had been dreading.

"What are you going to do now?"

Kerry paused before replying.

"I never meant to come back here, yet here I am. I suppose I wanted to make sure Kamitika and the cats were OK… I have no intention of staying. Please let me keep travelling with you."

Hikari thought Kerry should never have run away in the first place, but it didn't look like she was going to willingly return to her life as a princess. Also, she knew she would need as much help as possible if she was to defeat the Kelluas, and Kerry was a valuable help.

"Fine, you can still travel with me. But there's something I want you to do first."

Kerry looked worried.

"What do I have to do?"

"I want you to speak to Kamitika and Rhianna and at least let them know you're OK."

"No!" shouted Kerry.

A few of the people in the library glared at her in disapproval.

"No," Kerry repeated, in a quieter tone. "Kamitika maybe, but there's no way on Maysea I'm talking to Rhianna. It's been years since we last spoke."

"You have to, or I won't let you come with me," Hikari decided, folding her arms.

"You can't fight the Kelluas on your own!" argued Kerry.

Kerry glared angrily at Hikari for a second, and then reluctantly submitted.

"Alright, I'll do it. Kamitika first."

Hikari got up and walked towards Kamitika.

"Can I help you?" Kamitika asked in her usual shy voice.

"My friend here wants to speak to you about something. Can we go somewhere where no-one will hear us?" Hikari asked.

Kamitika looked worried as she looked at the hooded person standing next to Hikari.

"Ok, I guess... I can't leave the library for long though," she said quietly.

Hikari and Kerry followed Kamitika into the servant's quarter, and she brought them into a small room.

"This is my room," explained Kamitika.

The room was plain, with just a bed and a chest of drawers. A handmade stuffed dog was lying on the bed, and it looked as if it was made by someone who had never sewn before. One of its ears had fallen off, and the other was only hanging on by a few threads. Kerry walked over to it and picked it up.

"D... Don't touch that!" cried Kamitika.

"Why not? I made it for you, you know," said Kerry as she took down her hood.

Kamitika gasped when she realised it was Kerry.

"Kerry!" she exclaimed. "You came back!"

She hugged Kerry and started crying with relief.

"I knew you'd come back someday."

"Yeah... but I'm afraid I can't stay," said Kerry as she hugged Kamitika back.

"Why?" Kamitika said in despair.

"It's kind of a long story, but Snappytaps here is on a crazy quest to defeat a bunch of Kelluas, and I have decided to help her," said Kerry, pointing to Hikari.

Kamitika laughed and shook her head.

"That's so like you... Always doing the opposite of what a proper princess would do."

"Being a proper princess sucks," said Kerry bluntly.

Kerry set the stuffed dog back on the bed.

"Why don't you come with us, Kamitika?" said Kerry excitedly.

"Yeah!" agreed Hikari. "We'd love more people to come along with us."

Kamitika shook her head.

"I can't. I need to stay here and look after the library. Besides, I wouldn't be much good at fighting. I wish you two the best of luck though," she said as she hugged Kerry again, fiercely.

"See you soon."

"Yeah," said Kerry. "I'll be back."

Hikari and Kerry went back to the castle entrance hall, and Kamitika went back to the library. Kerry pulled her hood up again, and she still had one of the kitchen cats in her arms.

"Next, you speak to Rhianna," said Hikari, sternly.

"Fine…" moaned Kerry, who felt arguing with Hikari would be a waste of time. "Why do you care so much anyway?"

"You have a family who are alive and well, yet you chose to run away from them. I think while you're here you should at least talk to your sister," said Hikari.

"Follow me," Kerry said reluctantly as she started walking towards a grand staircase in the middle of the hall. "Her room is up here."

They got to the top of the stairs and Kerry stopped and peered down the corridor where Rhianna's room was. A uniformed guard stood at the entrance to the corridor.

"He won't let us in if he doesn't know who you are," whispered Hikari.

"Don't worry," replied Kerry. "I have it all sorted."

She let the cat in her arms run down the corridor. The guard screamed when he saw it.

Kerry laughed quietly.

"That guard has been working here for years. He's terrified of cats."

The cat seemed fascinated by the guard's boots, and he shrieked while trying to shake it off. Further up the corridor, a door opened.

"Rhianna…" whispered Kerry, as a figure walked out into the corridor.

Rhianna was tall and she had long, brown hair that almost reached her waist. She was wearing a full length button-through dress made of purple fabric, the image of a story book princess. There were dark circles under her eyes and she looked very annoyed.

"What is the meaning of this disturbance?" she demanded, glaring at the guard.

"Oh, Princess Rhianna. Sorry to disturb you," replied the guard in a flustered tone. "One of the kitchen cats got up here."

"Take it back down to the kitchen then, and don't make such a fuss," Rhianna said coldly.

"Y… Yes, your highness," stuttered the guard as he bent down and picked the cat up.

Kerry pulled Hikari behind a plant as the guard passed them and walked down the stairs, holding the cat at arm's length.

Rhianna sighed and shook her head before returning to her room.

"Let's go before he comes back," said Hikari, dragging Kerry to Rhianna's door.

Kerry knocked.

"I'm busy," said Rhianna from inside.

"I don't care," Kerry replied, and she pushed open the door and walked into the room.

Rhianna's room was huge. A four poster bed sat in the middle of the room, and the walls were covered in many different maps of the mainland and the island where Hikari was from. Rhianna was sitting at a mahogany desk surrounded by piles of textbooks. The book lying open on her desk was written entirely in Latin, and many pieces of paper were scattered around her with handwritten translations written on them in neat handwriting.

Kerry pulled her hood down, but Rhianna's reaction upon realising it was Kerry was very different to Kamitika's.

She stared at Kerry for a while before closing her book and folding her arms.

"What are you doing here?" she asked, with a hint of annoyance in her voice.

Yeah, I missed you too, thought Kerry sarcastically. *We haven't seen each other in over a year, and she still hates me.*

"At least you're actually speaking to me," said Kerry, and she sat down in an armchair.

"I asked you a question," said Rhianna.

Kerry wasn't exaggerating when she said her and Rhianna didn't get along, thought Hikari as she watched the sisters speak.

"I thought it would be nice to pop back home. See how the cats are doing, you know," said Kerry casually.

"If you don't intend to stay, hurry up and leave before Mother or Father catches you here," said Rhianna dismissively, and she reopened her Latin book and continued translating, ignoring Kerry.

Kerry clenched her fists in anger.

"I'm glad you care so much," she spat. "There Hikari, I spoke to her. I'm out."

Kerry departed the room and left Hikari awkwardly standing there.

"Who are you?" asked Rhianna, not taking her eyes off her book.

"I'm Hikari."

"Are you friends with Kerry?"

"Yes," said Hikari. "She's been kind to me."

Rhianna paused for a moment.

"Look after her, OK?" she said quietly. "She needs someone to guide her; she always runs into things head first without thinking of the consequences."

It seems deep down Rhianna really does care for Kerry.

"Why... Why don't you join us?" asked Hikari.

Kerry will kill me for this, but I really want these two to make up.

"Join you in what?" asked Rhianna.

"Some Kelluas destroyed my home and killed everyone who lived there except me. Now Kerry and I are travelling around the mainland until we find them and defeat them. The only thing is, we're both clueless. If we had someone with us who could read maps and stuff like that, it would be a great help."

Hikari realised the ridiculousness of her request. However, she could tell by looking that Rhianna was not as cold as she made out to be. She seemed exhausted and in desperate need of a break from her study.

"I... I don't think I could just up and leave the castle, even if I really wanted to," said Rhianna sadly. She felt the sincerity of Hikari's request and pitied her, but she was too tied to her royal duties.

"Why not? That's exactly what Kerry did. Aren't you sick of a life of Latin textbooks and never leaving the castle?"

What am I doing? I'm trying to convince the heir to the throne to pack up and leave her parents' castle. Why did I ever think this would work?

"It is customary for the heir of this kingdom to go on a journey at some stage before they inherit the throne, so they can gain a better understanding of their people. However, I doubt my parents would let me go when Kerry is still missing."

Rhianna stared longingly at one of the maps on her wall.

"I can name every single town, mountain and river in the mainland. I know the exact distance between any two towns. I know all this, yet I've never even left Alana. I've always wanted to leave, but I had too many responsibilities. "

Rhianna looked down sadly.

"When Kerry left, she asked me to join her. At that point I hadn't spoken to her in months, so I ignored her. There have been many times when I've wished I had joined her, but I was too overcome by envy of my sister. Instead, I decided I would stay and study as hard as I could to try and impress my parents."

I remember Kerry thought her parents loved Rhianna more than her, but Rhianna seems to think it's the other way round. I don't think things are as bad as they both think.

"Let's go and ask your parents then," said Hikari. "What's the worst they can do? Say no?"

Rhianna smiled.

"I guess that would be OK."

Rhianna led Hikari to the castle throne room. Kerry was nowhere to be seen, and Hikari guessed she was probably sulking in the kitchens and talking to the cats.

The throne room was just as Hikari expected it to be; a huge room filled with rows of chairs and two huge thrones at the front of the room. The King was pacing about in front of his chair, and he looked very annoyed. The Queen was trying her best to calm him down. The king was a large man with an impressively maintained beard, and his wife was also quite large in stature.

"What's wrong?" asked Rhianna when she saw her father.

"Rhianna, we need to talk to you..." said her mother, but her father interrupted before she could finish.

"He pulled out! The Prince of Shuri pulled out! Five months before the event!"

Hikari didn't understand what the King was talking about, but the look of sheer relief on Rhianna's face made it obvious this was good news for her.

"The wedding isn't taking place, Rhianna," said her mother solemnly.

"I see," replied Rhianna. "That's a shame."

Despite her words, Rhianna couldn't hide her joy.

"You would have made such a beautiful bride, too," the Queen said sadly.

Wait, what? Rhianna's the one getting married? Thought Hikari. *She's only eighteen! I understand why she looks so happy...*

"Mother, Father... I have a request to make," Rhianna said, changing the subject of the conversation.

"Does it have anything to do with that girl standing behind you?" said her father, who had calmed down a bit and was now sitting in his throne.

"Yes," began Rhianna. "I don't have to marry the Prince of Shuri anymore, so would it be possible for me to go travelling?"

The King and Queen were shocked at Rhianna's sudden request.

"I've stayed here for so long; I'd like to see more of the continent," Rhianna explained. "If I visited other kingdoms, I might learn more on how to be a good ruler."

The King didn't look too convinced.

"You're proposing to go travelling with this girl here?" he asked, looking at Hikari. "Rhianna, we've already lost one daughter…"

Rhianna nodded. She and Hikari had already worked out a story, because they were certain Rhianna wouldn't be allowed to go if her parents knew the journey would involve fighting against a dangerous ancient race. The story was simple: Hikari was a travelling merchant who needed help with selling goods across the continent. They decided not to mention Kerry would be coming along.

The King and Queen listened to Rhianna telling the story.

Hikari and Rhianna were sent outside to wait until the King and Queen made their decision. Hikari decided she would use this time to find out more about the Prince of Shuri.

"So, who is this Prince you were supposed to marry?" asked Hikari, aware of how nosy she was being.

"He's the second in line to the throne of a kingdom called Shuri, which is very rich in oil. Father wanted me to marry him, because of Shuri's wealth. I met him once and he is a nice enough person, but neither of us liked the idea of marrying someone we barely knew. Even if the marriage went ahead, we'd only see each other a few times a year until I inherit this throne. Royal marriages are based on politics, not love."

"You must be glad you got out of it," said Hikari.

"Indeed," replied Rhianna.

Before meeting Rhianna I asked myself "Who wouldn't want the life of a princess?" thought Hikari. *Now I'm beginning to see why she didn't want it. Constant studying, arranged marriages... I don't blame her for running away.*

A servant came to fetch Rhianna and Kerry.

"His Majesty will see you now," he said and he held the door open for them.

The King and Queen were sitting in their thrones and appeared much calmer than before.

"We have reached our decision," said the King.

Rhianna held her breath in anticipation.

"You can go," said the Queen, smiling.

Rhianna was elated. She abandoned all her princess etiquette and hugged her mother.

"Thank you so much!"

"Consider it our reward for being a good princess," said her father. "However, you can't go forever. We expect you to return and resume your role as heir. You are eighteen now; you may consider this the final road on your journey to adulthood."

Rhianna nodded.

"Yes, I won't be like Kerry," she promised.

"If you do see Kerry, please tell her to come back," said the Queen. "Tell her no-one is disappointed in her anymore. She can have a fresh start."

Rhianna knew it would take more than that to convince Kerry to go back, but she nodded anyway. The king turned his attention to Hikari, and the humble farm girl felt timid as he examined her.

"I see you are armed with a formidable weapon. I expect you to protect my daughter at all times," he said. "If you are negligent and she comes to harm, there will be severe consequences. Do you understand?"

"Yes sir," Hikari replied. "Leave it to me."

"I'll go and pack," said Rhianna enthusiastically. She ran out of the room and Hikari followed behind.

They went back to Rhianna's room, and she pulled a large leather bag out of the wardrobe.

"What equipment do you two already have?" Rhianna asked.

"A weapon each and the clothes on our backs," said Hikari. "Kerry has a water canteen we've been sharing."

Rhianna rolled her eyes.

"How did you ever think you were going to survive with just a weapon?" Rhianna asked, exasperated. She threw the bag over to Hikari.

"Hold that open."

Rhianna opened a drawer in her desk and handed Hikari a detailed handmade map of the Maysea Continent, including the island and the mainland. All towns, mountains, rivers and anything else of note were marked on it.

"Did you make this?" Hikari asked in amazement.

Rhianna nodded.

"You should have seen the map Kerry drew," she said, laughing. "The tutor was so annoyed and he made her do four more copies until he was satisfied."

Rhianna rummaged around her desk drawer some more and she pulled out a brass compass. She threw it to Hikari and she put it in the bag. Next she went over to her wardrobe, which was stuffed with an array of expensive clothes.

"I'll take clothes out of this wardrobe," said Rhianna. "You can go to the room at the end of this corridor. It's Kerry's old room, her clothes will be in there. Remember to bring clothes for all conditions."

Hikari nodded and went into Kerry's room.

Kerry's room had the same layout as Rhianna's, but instead of maps Kerry's walls were covered in sketches of the kitchen cats. Some of them looked really professional, and when Hikari looked at the signature in the corner of all the nice ones she saw they were painted by Kamitika. The others were by Kerry, and they were hardly recognisable as cats. They looked more like black blobs with legs and a tail.

Kerry's desk also had books on it, but they were far less advanced than Rhianna's.

Hikari opened Kerry's wardrobe. She took out an armful of clothes and brought them back to Rhianna. They put all the clothes into Rhianna's bag and fastened the top.

"I'm afraid you'll have to wear Kerry's clothes," said Rhianna apologetically. She hoisted the bag up on her back.

"Now we have to break the news to Kerry that you're coming along," said Hikari, grimacing.

They left Rhianna's room and Hikari found Kerry in the kitchens.

"What took you so long?" Kerry asked. "When are we going to read this Kellua book?"

With all this business of getting Kerry to talk to Rhianna and Kamitika, I completely forgot the only reason we came in here was to use the library, thought Hikari.

"I need to get out of here," said Kerry as she stood up. "The cook will probably be down any minute to start preparing dinner. I don't want her to see me!"

It's already evening? We've been in here so long?

Despite Hikari's silence, Kerry continued talking.

"The cook hates me. When I was a kid I always came down here to steal food."

Kerry and Hikari walked up the stairs to the entrance hall where Rhianna was waiting. Kerry scowled when she saw Rhianna standing with the bag on her back.

"What is she doing here?" Kerry asked Hikari through gritted teeth.

"She's coming with us," said Hikari. "She knows how to read maps and how to use a compass; I thought she'd be useful. Face it, Kerry. If we went on our own we'd get lost in the wilderness somewhere."

"If it's a problem you can stay here, Kerry," said Rhianna calmly.

"Why don't you stay here? Don't you have to study and be the perfect little princess you've always been? And what about the prince you were supposed to marry?" shouted Kerry.

Thankfully there were no people in the entrance hall to overhear her. Hikari knew if Kerry's parents realised she was in the castle they wouldn't let her leave.

"The wedding is off," explained Rhianna. "And unlike you, I actually asked permission to leave."

Kerry turned to Hikari.

"Did you suggest this?" she asked angrily.

"Yes. I did," replied Hikari.

Kerry stamped her foot in rage.

"Fine, whatever. Don't expect me to make friends with her," she said coldly.

It looks like it's going to take a lot of work to get these two to like each other again. Kerry seems to be the main problem.

"Let's read that book and get out of this stupid city," snapped Kerry, and she stormed off towards the library.

Kamitika smiled as they entered the library. Everyone else had left, and the library was empty.

"Kerry! Hikari!" she said happily. "Princess Rhianna!" She quickly curtsied.

"The book you requested earlier is on the table over there," said Kamitika as she pointed towards a table surrounded by soft chairs.

"Thank you," said Hikari, and the three girls sat down at the table. They flipped through the book and Rhianna wrote down anything that looked important in a notebook.

They read the book for what felt like ages and Rhianna looked over her notes.

Origins of the Kellua Tribe

In the past, humans knew how to harness magic powers. Some became obsessed and used it to conduct barbarous experiments. One man desired to use magic for offensive purposes and successfully combined his own powers with an evil spirit. In the process he lost much of his humanity. Soon many followed his example and these people became known as 'Kelluas', an ancient word that translates as 'others'. They became isolated from the rest of society.

A Kellua's Abilities

Kelluas have the ability to float up to a metre off the ground. The purpose of this ability is to protect their head from being hit, as the back of their head is their one known weak spot. They attack by shooting colourful orbs of energy which can inflict tremendous damage, depending on the strength of the Kellua projecting them. Kelluas can become human again if they release the evil spirit that indwells within them.

The Kellua War

The humans agreed to live peacefully side by side with the Kelluas, but some of the humans were afraid of the destructive potential of their power. Additionally, the human settlements were getting overcrowded and they wanted the Kelluas' land. They began to fight against them. The Kelluas were much stronger than the humans, so the humans gathered more people from all around the continent to join the fight. The Kelluas were greatly outnumbered and ultimately they were defeated. The humans sealed the powers of the remaining Kellua and they scattered throughout the land in a weakened state. They have not been sighted for decades.

"This information is useful and everything, but it doesn't give us any clue as to where the Kelluas could be located now," said Hikari.

"They are probably trying to reclaim the land we humans stole from them," said Rhianna thoughtfully.

"And we still don't know anything about the 'experiment' Kyros and Michius were talking about," said Kerry. It was the first time she had spoken since entering the library.

"Also, the book doesn't mention anything about Kelluas having the ability to teleport, yet we saw Kyros and Michius teleport right in front of us," added Hikari.

"Perhaps it's a new skill they've learned," suggested Rhianna.

Hikari couldn't help but feel disappointed. "This is getting us nowhere."

"We still have a few hints," said Rhianna reassuringly. "They attacked Honif, but they left the other two towns on the island alone."

"There aren't any little kids in Dunin," said Kerry. "They wouldn't target there."

"But there are kids in Port Gorm," Hikari pointed out, remembering the girl who spoke to her and Kerry.

"Exactly, but they left Port Gorm alone," said Rhianna. "They seem to only want to attack small villages. It's probably so they don't draw too much attention to themselves. After all, they know what will happen if they simply run in and start attacking cities. The past will repeat itself, and the humans will rise up and defeat them."

"I intend on doing just that," said Hikari determinately.

"But why did they destroy Honif? Why not just take Hikari's sister and run?" said Kerry, puzzled.

"They probably wanted to kill all possible witnesses," said Rhianna.

"It seems they're heartlessly over-cautious when they're carrying out their plans," said Hikari in dismay. "Also, my sister had a name. She was called Liza."

Rhianna looked up at the antique grandfather clock at the side of the library and saw it had struck eleven.

"It's getting late," she said. "You can stay at the castle tonight Hikari, and we can work out our plan of action tomorrow. I'm too tired to think."

The girls set the book back on the table and walked out of the library. Kamitika had already gone to bed. Hikari slept in one of the guest rooms, wearing one of Kerry's nightgowns. It was a big change from the straw mattress she was used to sleeping on in Honif – even the guest rooms were nearly as large as her old house.

This could be our last night sleeping in comfort for a while. When we resume travelling we may have to sleep outdoors. I wonder how Princess Rhianna will cope.

I hope we can get more information on where the Kelluas will strike next. We need to warn people about them so they can protect their children.

Before long, Hikari fell into a deep sleep.

***

Where am I?

She tried to look around her, but she couldn't see anything except a strange white mist.

A figure began to appear from within the mist.

Who is that? Wait….

The figure was that of a young girl. She opened her mouth, but Hikari couldn't hear what she was saying. She began to fade back into the mist.

Wait! Liza! Don't go! I don't want you to leave!

***

Hikari spent the rest of the night in a restless, dreamless state of half-sleep.

Chapter 5

Hikari and Rhianna met in the library in the morning.

"I thought about it overnight, and I think our best chance of catching the Kelluas is to travel to small villages and hope we get lucky," said Rhianna. "It doesn't look like we'll get any more information by staying here."

Hikari nodded.

"Where's the nearest village?" asked Hikari.

"There's a village called Azure Falls to the west of here," said Rhianna, without even having to look at the map. "If we leave now, we should get there by nightfall."

They said farewell to Kamitika before leaving the library.

"Where's Kerry?" Hikari asked. "Is she still in bed? I haven't seen her this morning."

"I think I've got a good idea of where she'll be," Rhianna smiled. "Follow me."

Rhianna led Hikari back through the entrance hall towards another room. This room was not as large or grand as the library. There were rows of plain wooden pews facing a wooden cross attached to the far wall. There were stained glass windows on either side of the cross, painting the floor with a palette of colours as the sun shone into the room. It created an inviting atmosphere, and Hikari didn't feel as out of place as she did in the rest of the castle.

Just as Rhianna had predicted, Kerry was at the front of the room talking to an older man with a white collar. She noticed Rhianna and Hikari standing there, and ran up to them.

"I was getting the minister to bless our journey before we set out," she said. "He promised not to let mother and father know I was here."

So Kerry's one of those fairy tale believers as well... Hikari thought.

"Do you want to pray together before we set out?" Kerry asked earnestly.

Rhianna shook her head.

"We need to get going before it gets too late. I'm sure you've done enough to cover all three of us," Rhianna replied, rolling her eyes.

"Always a pessimist," Kerry grumbled as they left the room.

When they were outside and finally beyond the castle gates Rhianna smiled, feeling free for the first time in her life as a princess. Kerry was still refusing to talk to Rhianna, and she wouldn't even walk beside her.

They stopped off at a market place and bought some food for the journey, including freshly baked bread rolls and bunches of grapes. Kerry had found a small bag in her room, and they filled it with food. Rhianna had taken a sword from the castle armoury to use if she ever needed to fight. Rhianna had also been given a large amount of money from her parents that would be more than enough to fund their journey.

Hikari was extremely grateful she had met these two. Otherwise, she would probably still be wandering the island hopelessly depressed, with nothing but a hoe to defend herself with.

Once they had bought all they needed, they headed west out of Alana. The road between Alana and Azure Falls was quiet, and apart from one man on horseback, the girls didn't encounter anyone. The path led into a dense forest full of tall oak trees, and Rhianna consulted her map.

"We'll have to be careful," she warned as she looked at the map. "I wrote this forest's name in red ink, which means it has quite a few monsters living in it."

The trees of the forest surrounded the small path. Hikari glanced at the trees anxiously, waiting for a monster to appear. The trees were so dense that little light passed through to the path, and the darkness was unsettling. They walked on further into the forest, and something jumped out in front of them. Kerry screamed and hastily drew her sword, but they had only startled a rabbit. It ran off into the trees and Kerry turned to Rhianna.

"Some kind of map that is," she sneered. "It's making us paranoid over monsters when there's nothing but animals in this forest."

"Are you forgetting I've never actually been here before?" replied Rhianna in disgust. "This map is based on information I read in the castle library. Get annoyed at the authors of those books, not me."

"Why did we bring your stupid map anyway?" asked Kerry. "Why didn't we bring something by an actual cartographer?"

Hikari was about to try and break up the fight, but a growling from behind the trees quickly silenced them.

A creature leapt out of the trees and bore its teeth at the girls. At first glance Hikari thought it was a wolf, but normal wolves don't have piercing red eyes and fangs dripping with purple saliva. It was certainly a monster, and it was clear it was acting upon its instincts: attack anything that moves.

"Satisfied?" Rhianna asked Kerry as she drew her sword. Kerry ignored her and drew her own sword. Hikari followed suit and they all ran at the monster with weapons in hand.

It ran at Kerry and tried to bite her legs, but she nimbly jumped backwards and avoided the attack. Rhianna had never been in a proper combat situation before, but she soon adjusted. The monster was vicious but it had a terrible sense of direction, and the girls ran in circles around it to confuse it. Rhianna and Hikari brought their weapons down on the creature and killed it instantly. Its corpse quickly disintegrated into the ground.

"That's gross..." said Kerry.

"At least it proved my map was correct," said Rhianna as she returned her sword to the belt of her dress.

Will these two ever stop fighting? Maybe it wasn't such a good idea to bring Rhianna along. But we'd literally be lost without her.

An awkward silence filled the air and they continued walking. After many hours the trees thinned out and the village of Azure Falls came into view. It was made up of several log cabins and huge logs were piled up in front of many of the buildings. Active chimneys filled the air with a smoky smell.

"I remember briefly learning about this place," said Rhianna. "Timber is their main industry. The most common job around here is being a lumberjack."

It wasn't hard to see how the village got its name. It was built in front of a large cliff, and a clear blue waterfall flowed from the top of the cliff into a small lake below.

There was no one about outside, but through the windows of the cabins Hikari could see the glow of fireplaces. The largest cabin was right next to the lake, and a sign saying 'Travellers Welcome' was hung on the door.

The girls made their way to the cabin and knocked on the door, and an old woman opened it. She was dressed in woollen clothing and her hair was paper white.

"Oh, are you travellers?" she asked kindly. "Do you need to stay here tonight?"

"Yes please, that would be lovely," said Rhianna.

They walked inside the cabin. It was warm from the heat of the fire, and several animal skin rugs were laid out on the floor. There was a pot hanging over the fireplace with some sort of soup cooking in it, and the smell gave the room a welcoming atmosphere.

"Take a seat in those chairs by the fireplace and I'll give you some soup," said the old lady, pointing to three armchairs.

"It's ok, honestly," began Hikari. "We have our own food."

"No, no," insisted the old lady. "There's plenty to go round. We normally have more guests, but the ghost that appeared yesterday made them leave in a hurry."

"Ghost?" asked Kerry, immediately interested.

"Things have been going missing and people have reported seeing mysterious shadows at night. Gossip spreads fast, and now the entire village is terrified," explained the old woman fearfully.

I don't believe in ghosts, thought Rhianna. *However, I do believe in Kelluas. And this whole 'ghost' story stinks of Kellua involvement.*

"Thanks for the information," said Rhianna. "We'll take some soup, please."

The woman smiled and the girls sat down in the armchairs.

"My name is Ester, by the way," said the woman.

"I'm Hikari, and this is Rhianna and Kerry," explained Hikari.

Ester gave them each a bowl of soup, before going off to prepare a room for them.

"So, what do you make of this ghost?" Kerry asked as she blew on her soup.

"It's probably the Kelluas," replied Rhianna.

"Are there any little kids in this village?" asked Kerry.

"How should I know?" snapped Rhianna.

"Geez, I was just asking," said Kerry.

I can't stand much more of this... thought Hikari as she ate in silence. *If we're going to see if this ghost really is a Kellua, they can't be constantly arguing.*

When they had finished eating Ester came in and told them their room was ready. Kerry and Rhianna started walking towards the room, but Hikari stopped them.

"We need to talk outside," Hikari demanded.

Kerry and Rhianna followed Hikari outside, worried about what Hikari had to speak to them about. Hikari leaned against the outside of the cabin and faced them. It was cold and their breath hung in the air around them. The moon reflected on the pool at the bottom of the waterfall, the pale light shining on the calm waters.

"You two are going to sort out your differences right now, and I'm not letting you come with me unless you make up," said Hikari bluntly.

Kerry snorted with laughter.

"Rhianna's a stuck up, know-it-all princess," she said.

Rhianna glared at Kerry.

"You're an immature, stupid child who thinks nothing of her duties as a princess," she retaliated.

"Shut up, both of you!" screamed Hikari. "All you do is fight! You both have different ideas and values, but that's ok!" yelled Hikari. "I would never expect two sisters to be exactly the same as each other! But you need to get over your differences. Kerry, you should never have run away from Alana. Rhianna, you shouldn't have stopped talking to Kerry merely because you were jealous of the attention she got from your parents. You both have faults, suck it up and deal with it!"

Kerry and Rhianna were shocked speechless. They had never seen Hikari so worked up.

"I'm sorry, but seeing you two fight really, really irritates me," Hikari continued. "You're so lucky. You have parents and a sister who are alive and well. Something I will never have again."

Hikari started getting tearful.

"What if one of you was to die? What if the last thing you ever did was argue? Appreciate what you have and stop being so petty!"

She paused to wipe tears away from her eyes.

"If you two can't make up, you might as well leave now. Kerry can go back to living with stray cats on the island. Rhianna can go back to the castle. I don't care what you do, as long as you stay out of my sight and stop distracting me from avenging my sister, whom I'd given anything in the world to have back in my life."

Hikari had said all she wanted to say. She marched back into the cabin and left Kerry and Rhianna standing outside. They stood in silence, unsure of what to say to each other.

"You know..." Rhianna began quietly after an awkward minute of silence. "When you asked me to run away with you, I really wanted to go. However, I was too proud to start speaking to you again after all that time ignoring you. The truth is, Kerry... I've missed you. I know it didn't seem that way when you came to my room yesterday, but Hikari has made me realise I need to let go of my stupid pride and accept you as my sister."

Kerry was shocked. She had always thought Rhianna hated her, and she also thought by running away she had done Rhianna a favour. It had never occurred to Kerry that Rhianna might have actually missed her.

Kerry thought of Hikari, and how upset she was over losing Liza.

"Rhianna, I'm sorry," she said. "I'm sorry for being an idiot. I always did whatever I wanted, and I never stopped to think how it would affect you. "

Rhianna laughed.

"Hikari's right. We're both idiots."

Kerry threw her arms around Rhianna, and the two sisters hugged for the first time in years.

"Can we go inside now?" asked Kerry. "It's so cold; I can't feel my fingers anymore."

"Yeah, we can't let Hikari stay warm and cosy inside while we're out here freezing!"

The sisters grinned at each other and went back inside the cabin. They were surprised at how easy it had been to forgive each other once they'd let go of the petty resentment that had built up over the years.

Hikari had meant to stay awake to see if Kerry and Rhianna would make up, but the journey had tired her out and she quickly fell asleep. And as she did, she started to dream.

***

What…? Where am I?

I'm near a river. And there are two small children getting water from the river with two old buckets.

Wait… Those kids….

The older one with brown hair. Isn't that... me? And the smaller one is Liza.

Hikari tried to call out, but her body wouldn't respond. She was paralyzed by the poignant recollection.

No! I don't want this! Why can't I wake up? I don't want to remember this!

***

When morning came, Hikari was awoken by sunlight streaming through the window. She rubbed her eyes and opened them to see Rhianna sitting on the bed closest to the door, sorting through her bag. Rhianna noticed Hikari was awake.

"Good morning," said Rhianna, smiling. "Are you OK? You looked like you were having a bad dream last night."

"I'm fine," replied Hikari, forcing a smile. She didn't want to talk about her dream, even to Rhianna. She decided to change the subject. "Where's Kerry?"

Rhianna laughed.

"She was going to wait until you woke up, but the smell of Ester cooking breakfast was too tempting and she started without us."

"Did you two make up?" asked Hikari, feeling hopeful.

"Yes, we did. Thank you, Hikari," said Rhianna. "You helped us realise how petty we were when we fought."

Mission accomplished. What a relief.

"Glad to hear it. Now, what was that you said about breakfast?"

Hikari and Rhianna went into the main room where Kerry was already sitting in a chair eating freshly baked bread and raspberry jam.

"Snappytaps! You're awake!" said Kerry, nearly choking on her food. "Did Rhianna tell you? We decided to stop fighting after you spoke to us last night!"

Hikari took a piece of the bread and sat down.

"Yes, she told me. I'm so happy for you both."

Now they're friends, and their constant arguing won't annoy me anymore. Everyone's a winner!

***

Saya kicked Kyros, who was sleeping on the ground.

"Get up, you lazy sloth!" she yelled. "We're out of food, go and steal some."

Kyros dragged himself up. He hated sleeping outside in the open; it made him feel sore all over.

"Why can't you get food?" he moaned.

"Because the Superior's cross with you for screwing up the last mission," laughed Saya. "You have to do what I say as punishment."

"Fine."

Kyros was even more afraid of the Superior than he was of Saya. Out of the five surviving Kelluas, he was the youngest and the weakest. He feared what the Superior would do to him if he failed another mission.

He groaned and walked the short distance through the woods between Azure Falls and where he and Saya were hiding. The Superior's experiment to regain their power was going well, and as part of it they had gained the ability to teleport. However, he had not been able to master the skill like the others had, and he had to rely on embarrassingly clinging to them while they teleported him to wherever he needed to go. Even the others had some limitations: in their weakened state, they didn't have much stamina and they had to rest in between uses of teleportation.

He had been hiding out with Saya for what felt like an eternity, even though it had only been a couple of days. Their target was a young girl living in Azure Falls, who was about four years old. Kyros didn't even know why a young child was so important to the Superior's experiment. Saya knew, but she refused to tell him and laughed at his ignorance.

Kyros hated the experiment. Yes, it had given him new powers. But at the same time, it had almost gotten him killed twice.

He and Saya had been ordered to discreetly kidnap the child and not to attack anyone unless they were confronted. The all-out attack approach had failed miserably in Honif, so a different approach was needed. Kyros now understood why no-one liked to let him make the plans.

Kyros decided to stop feeling sorry for himself and get on with the task of stealing. He saw a young couple leave their cabin with axes in their hands, off to cut some trees. He took this as an opportunity to snatch up their food. They had left a window open and Kyros managed to squeeze his way in. Once he was inside and made sure he was alone and then started pulling food out of the cupboards.

He had nearly acquired all he needed when a small voice interrupted him.

"Excuse me, are you a robber?" a little girl asked, eyes wide with fear.

The girl had curly long brown hair that was tied back in a messy ponytail and she was wearing a woollen dress.

Oh no, thought Kyros. *I forgot this is where the girl we were targeting lived. Hey, wait a second....*

"Yup, I'm a robber," he said, "and now you're coming with me!"

Kyros went to grab the child and run off with her, but before he got the chance she opened her mouth and screamed.

"YUTI, WE'RE BEING ROBBED!!!"

As quick as lightning, a boy ran into the room. He looked about eighteen, and he had spiky blonde hair. He had a grimace on his face.

"Trying to rob us, are you?" he asked Kyros.

Double oh no.

"No...I was just..." but Kyros stopped talking. There was no point in defending himself when he was standing there with an armful of stuff he had taken from their cupboards.

Meanwhile, Kerry, Rhianna and Hikari heard the child's scream all the way from Ester's house.

"Do you think it's the Kelluas?" asked Kerry, jumping off her seat.

"Only one way to find out," said Hikari, and she ran out the door.

They raced to the cabin where Kyros was. Hikari felt an intense abhorrence as she looked upon her sister's killer.

"Oh, look who it is," sneered Kerry.

Kyros began to panic.

It's not my day, is it? I'm surrounded by people who want to kill me. This really isn't good.

He ran out the door and made a dash for the trees.

"Saya!" he screamed.

He hated to admit it, but Saya was far superior to him when it came to battle strength. He would be defeated straight away without her.

Rhianna, Kerry and Hikari drew their weapons and faced him.

"I knew you'd come here," said Rhianna.

The blonde boy ran out of his cabin armed with an axe.

Saya, where are you? The one time when I actually want to see your annoying face...

With that thought, Saya broke through the trees.

"Who's that? Another Kellua?" yelled Kerry.

"Yup," said Saya, "And you'd better be prepared to die!"

Saya started floating off the ground and hurled pink balls of energy at the humans. Kyros quickly followed suit.

The blonde boy ran forward with his axe and lunged at Saya, but she floated out of the way and threw an energy ball at him. He didn't quite dodge it and it singed his trousers as it passed. He continued to swing his axe in her direction.

Wow. He's strong, thought Rhianna as she started swinging her sword in Kyros' direction.

Apart from a bit of play fighting with the castle guards when she was little, this was the first time Rhianna had been involved in actual combat. She quickly got used to it, although she remained on guard at all times. She had a duty to return to her parents unharmed.

Kerry turned to the blonde haired boy.

"Go for the blue haired one first," she said. "He's weaker."

Saya laughed at this.

"So true, little girl."

The boy scowled.

"I'll do what I want," he replied in a gruff voice.

Hikari, Kerry and Rhianna all attacked Kyros, while the blonde boy went for Saya. Their agility was pushed to the limit as they tried to simultaneously doge orbs while remaining close enough to attack. They all managed to land hits, and Kyros quickly fell to the ground.

Saya was also hit pretty hard, but she managed to stay standing.

"You're stronger than you look…" she said, breathing rapidly. "Farewell for now. We'll meet again."

Saya teleported.

"Wait!" Kyros called desperately as he lay helplessly on the ground. "You know I can't teleport on my own! Saya!"

But Saya was already gone.

I'm doomed. Completely doomed.

"That was heartless, even for a Kellua…" remarked Kerry. "Abandoning an injured ally!"

The blonde boy walked up to Kyros.

"P – please don't kill me," begged Kyros.

"Then tell me what you were doing stealing food from our cabin," the boy demanded.

"I was hungry, OK?" said Kyros as he staggered to his feet. "Look at me. I'm useless. If I said I was going to leave the Kelluas, what would you say?"

The girls were taken aback by this unexpected question.

"Every time I get sent on a mission, I end up getting defeated. And as you saw, the other Kelluas don't really care what happens to me," he continued.

Kerry hesitated, unsure if he was lying or not.

"If you're so useless," she asked hesitantly, "Why do you get sent on all these missions?"

"Because it doesn't matter to them if I die or not," Kyros replied bluntly. "I'm expendable. If I refuse to follow orders, they'll kill me anyway. I'm asking you for mercy. If I were to turn my back on the Kelluas now, and walk away, would you leave me alone?"

"You killed my sister," said Hikari, her voice filled with hatred.

"Hikari..." began Rhianna. "I understand your anger. But it seems to me it's the more powerful Kelluas are the real villains responsible for Liza's death. Kyros here is just a pawn. I think we should let him go."

"But he's still a Kellua! Even if he's weak, he has the power to kill people!" Hikari protested.

"If that is what concerns you, have no fear. I will surrender my powers," said Kyros calmly.

Before the girls could say any more, he thrust both of his hands into the air. A blue light surrounded both his hands, getting brighter and brighter as he focused his energy. Beads of sweat appeared on his forehead as he struggled to maintain the action. With a final thrust of effort, the light dissipated into the air. His energy totally drained, he fell to his knees. He was completely purged of his Kellua identity. His blue hair had transformed to a natural shade of blonde.

"Did he... Did he remove his powers?" said Hikari in disbelief.

Kyros nodded weakly before collapsing on the ground.

"What is he?" said the blonde boy in disbelief.

"We'll explain later, but this guy needs help," said Kerry, as she and Rhianna lifted an unconscious Kyros off the ground.

They brought him into Ester's cabin, and Ester gasped in shock upon seeing the unconscious Kyros.

"What happened?"

"He's a traveller. I think he's exhausted," said Hikari.

Something tells me 'He's a Kellua who removed his powers' wouldn't go over so well, thought Hikari.

It's so strange. I wanted nothing more than for Kyros to die, yet here we all are helping him. I suppose it's like Rhianna said. The Kelluas at the top are using Kyros as their pawn. I shouldn't kill him. However, I'm not going to make friends with him. The sooner we can get away from here and get on the trail of those truly responsible for Liza's death, the better.

Ester took Kyros into one of the guest rooms so she could assess if he needed any aid. The girls and the blonde boy were left alone as they sat around the fireplace.

"Can someone tell me what just happened?" the boy asked with a bewildered tone.

"Before we start explaining, what's your name?" asked Kerry in a friendly tone.

"Yuti," he mumbled. "That guy... He wasn't just robbing us. Before I burst in the room, I heard him say something about taking Ailsa with him."

"Ailsa?" asked Kerry, confused.

"The couple who live in that cabin are my adoptive parents," said Yuti. "Ailsa is their real daughter."

"She must be the reason they came here," said Kerry.

"I don't understand," said Yuti, annoyed. "What is a Kellua?"

"Kelluas are members of an ancient tribe that can use combat magic, and they also have the ability to float. The humans stole their homeland centuries ago, and they're trying to get it back," explained Rhianna.

"How does Ailsa come into this?" asked Yuti.

"The Kelluas are doing some sort of experiment, but we don't really know what it is or what it is for. However, we do know they need a child to complete the experiment," said Hikari. "Kyros... he killed my sister. So now we're trying to defeat the Kelluas before they harm any more kids."

"You're telling me that man wanted to kill Ailsa?" said Yuti, trembling with rage.

"Please, don't get angry with him. Get angry with his superiors," begged Kerry.

"Right then," said Yuti determinately. "Tell Ailsa and her parents I'm going to track down these Kelluas."

Yuti got up, and grabbed his axe from where he set it down in the corner of the room.

"Wait!" yelled Kerry, and she stood up. "You don't know where you're going! Why don't you come with us?"

Yuti grunted.

"I think I'm better on my own than with a bunch of girls tagging along," he snapped, before walking out the door.

"Geez," said Kerry as she sat down again. "He didn't even listen to the whole story. He has no clue how to find them."

"It's his fault for being an idiot," said Hikari, not really bothered.

"When Kyros recovers, we should get some information out of him about the experiment," Rhianna added.

Kerry and Hikari agreed, and they waited for over an hour before Ester came back in and told them Kyros had finally woken up.

"May we see him?" asked Hikari.

"Yes, but not for too long. He needs to rest," said Ester.

It shouldn't take long. He will tell us what he knows, and then we can be on our way, thought Hikari, who wasn't looking forward to seeing him again.

They went into Kyros' room, which contained a bed and a lit fireplace.

"Please don't hurt me. I made myself human. What more do you want?" asked Kyros when he saw the girls come in.

"Information," said Kerry, bluntly. "Tell us all you know about your superiors and this 'experiment'."

"Fine," he said. "But I don't know that much."

"Then reveal what you know," said Rhianna.

Should I lie, or should I tell the truth? thought Kyros. *I could easily throw them off the others' scent with false information. But do I really want to protect the others? They used me.*

I'll tell them the truth. It's not like the experiment matters to me anymore. I'm human now.

Kyros began to speak.

"There are five of us. The girl you saw earlier was Saya. She's the only female Kellua left. The person I was with on the island is Michius. There's also Oden, whom you haven't met yet. He has green hair, and he's second in command. Finally, there's the Superior. He has black hair, and I don't even know his real name. He's a very mysterious individual, and he's also the one who gathered us survivors together."

"As for the experiment, the Superior wants to reclaim the power and land you humans stole from us years ago, but he knows we're not powerful enough right now to do it. In the ruins of one of our old villages, he found a book on how to restore our once legendary powers through a series of experiments. The first one we tried was teleportation. For it, we had to track down a type of flower that only grew in the Northern Mountains and eat it. That one was a moderate success. We gained limited teleportation powers, but we didn't find enough flowers to perfect that skill."

The girls listened in interest as Kyros continued.

"What the Superior wants more than anything is invincibility. If we are invincible humans can do nothing to stop us. To achieve it he said he needs a human child under eight years old, but we don't know exactly what he needs from them. He stressed the child needs to be brought to him alive."

"You messed that one up," sneered Hikari, who still didn't feel ready to trust or forgive Kyros for Liza's accidental death.

"Hikari…" Rhianna said kindly. "If he's genuinely ashamed of what he did, we should try our best to be forgiving."

"I know I did a terrible thing, and I'm truly sorry," said Kyros. "Please believe me when I say I didn't mean to kill your sister. To help you seek your revenge, I can predict the others' next move. They won't return here, because people saw you fighting us in broad daylight. I'm sure Saya will be in huge trouble with the Superior when she gets back for blowing our cover. We were supposed to be keeping a low profile until we regained the full strength of our powers. Pretty soon, rumours will start to spread that the Kelluas are back. Anyway, the next target is a village called Tura. It was our backup plan if we failed to capture a child here."

"Isn't that a village to the north of here?" asked Rhianna.

"Yes," he said. "It's quite a long journey."

Rhianna pulled her map out.

"Let's see..." she said, while pinpointing their current position on the map.

"We'll have to walk through the northern part of the forest for about a day, and then we'll arrive at a large city called Alburn. From there it's about another day's walk to Tura. It's in the foothills of the Northern Mountains, and it's pretty cold at this time of year," said Rhianna.

"Do we have warm clothes packed in that huge bag of yours?" asked Kerry.

"Yes," replied Rhianna. "I'm afraid you'll have to wear clothes belonging to Kerry, Hikari."

Hikari laughed.

"Better that than freezing to death."

"That's all I can tell you," said Kyros.

"Thanks," said Kerry. "It will help us a lot. What will you do now, Kyros?"

"I don't know," he said honestly. "I suppose I'll find a town somewhere where I can work to earn my keep."

"Make sure you stay out of trouble. And don't even think about re-joining the Kellua," warned Hikari. She had considered asking Kyros to join them, but she didn't want to travel with her sister's killer, even if it wasn't entirely his fault. Hikari marvelled at how easily Kerry and Rhianna were able to forgive Kyros but then again, they were not saddled by the burden of a personal vendetta.

The girls left Kyros alone and went back into the main room. They decided, because it was close to nightfall, they would stay one more night in Azure Falls before beginning their journey to Tura. They were eating dinner when someone knocked on the front door.

Ester opened it, and it was Ailsa's parents. They looked very worried.

"Ester, have you seen Yuti?" the woman asked, close to tears, "Apparently he was involved in a fight against a robber earlier, and now we can't find him."

Great. Now we have to explain to her that her adopted son has left the village armed with an axe to go off and chase some monsters, thought Rhianna.

"He said he was going on a journey," Rhianna explained carefully. "He'll be back soon."

The woman looked even more worried.

"A journey where? To do what? Who with?" asked the man.

"We don't know for sure," said Rhianna, "Something about protecting Ailsa from monsters. If we find him while we're travelling, we'll do our best to send him home."

The parents looked grateful, but still concerned.

"Thank you. If you see him, please tell him we love him and want him to come home" the father said before putting his arm around Yuti's mother and walking her back to their cabin, where Ailsa was waiting.

Chapter 6

Near Azure Falls, in a city called Alburn, a boy sat looking out of a window onto the paved streets below. In front of him was a potter's wheel, with a lump of wet, grey clay on it. Several similar looking lumps of clay had been discarded at his feet, all failed attempts at making cups.

The boy was an apprentice of a skilled potter, and he had been learning pottery for nearly a year. However, he couldn't do it. His master, the potter, could make perfectly shaped vases, plates and bowls in a matter of seconds. The boy would spend hours on one measly cup and it would always turn out unusable.

He threw the piece he was currently moulding onto the floor in frustration. He knew what his master would say when he saw the mess he had made.

"Noi, I've been training you for months. Why is it you still can't do anything with a piece of clay?"

Noi could imagine his master saying those exact words. He'd said them many times before.

Noi was seventeen and he was tall and thin. He had short brown hair and a fringe that used to flop over his face until his master ordered him to get it cut. He told him potters can't produce quality pieces if they're blinded by their hair. Noi couldn't produce quality pieces, fringe or no fringe.

Noi had grown up in an orphanage. He didn't know anything about his parents, but he didn't really care. He knew they were either dead or they didn't want to look after him, so he had no desire of running away to try and find his parents, as many of the boys in the orphanage had done in the past. His orphanage had been overcrowded, with an age range spanning from abandoned new-born babies to eighteen year old adolescents.

Just like any establishment with numerous youths, bullying occurred frequently. He was thankful he didn't fall into any of the 'bullying categories'; too thin, too fat, too tall, too small, too weak... the list goes on.

Despite the obvious setbacks, the orphanage wasn't that bad. He was clothed, he never starved, he was educated, and he even got a small gift at Christmas. He had shared a room with six other boys and although he wouldn't really call them his friends, they weren't bad people. The orphanage was run by monks in the local monastery, and only boys were allowed.

One of Noi's fondest memories of his time in the orphanage was sneaking out with the boys from his room and trying to get into the girls' orphanage, a place run by nuns. Their plan failed miserably when a nun caught them trying to climb over the railings by the girls' orphanage and sent them back in disgrace. The abbot had punished them severely, but all the younger boys looked at Noi and his friends with admiration for daring to disobey the abbot's strict rules.

Life in the orphanage was good, but Noi had one problem with it. It was desperately boring. Every day was the same; prayers at dawn, lessons in the morning, jobs around the monastery until evening and going to bed at nine o'clock (which he thought was ridiculously early). On Sundays they were expected to attend church at least twice a day. Whenever a respected potter came to the orphanage looking for a new apprentice, Noi was first in line. He thought an apprenticeship would be the perfect opportunity to break away from his mundane life at the orphanage.

He was wrong. It was a change of lifestyle, yes, but Noi hated it. He found he actually missed his old life in the orphanage.

He shook his head and took another lump of clay from the sack beside him. He gritted his teeth and slapped the wet clay on the potter's wheel, determined to stop feeling sorry for himself. He started spinning the wheel and tried to make a half decent cup.

***

We've been walking for so long... thought Kerry as she half-heartedly dragged her feet along the ground. *I wish we had a horse and cart. Then this whole journey would be much quicker. In fact, someone should make a cart that can run on its own, without a horse. But even I know that's impossible.*

Rhianna and Hikari were walking ahead of her at a much quicker pace.

Where do they get their energy?

Kerry was supposed to be watching out for monsters, like the one that had attacked them on their way to Azure Falls, but she was too tired to do anything except sluggishly put one foot in front of the other.

Hikari turned around and yelled at Kerry.

"The faster you walk, the faster we will reach our destination!" she called, grinning.

Kerry moaned and ran to catch up with Hikari and Rhianna.

God, give me strength... I hate walking. I really do.
***

In the evening, Noi went to the Alburn Market in the centre of town. To his despair, he had not been able to make a cup. He had moulded it for hours and produced something semi-useable, but he dropped it on his way to fire it. He had never been so close to crying in his life. The potter was enraged at his foolish mistake and sent him out of the house in disgrace to buy things from the market, because that was all he was useful for.

The market was on the edge of the city, and you could see the woods beyond stretching far into the horizon. Noi had never left Alburn, but he had always wondered what lay beyond the woods. Perhaps he would know if he had actually listened during his geography lessons in the orphanage, but he hated geography. He liked the idea of travelling and seeing new places without having to follow a map. To him a map was a piece of paper with meaningless squiggles and icons etched all over it.

He bought the items his master wanted, and he was about to head back to the workshop when a strange looking girl with purple hair and a sword came up to him. She was panting and she looked as if she had been on her feet all day.

"Inn... where... now..." she panted in incoherent English.

Two more girls, also carrying weapons, followed behind her.

"Geez, Kerry," said the tallest girl, "How can you be so tired?"

The purple-haired girl glared at her.

"I had to run half the time to catch up with you two," she snapped. "Why must you walk so fast?"

"Why must you walk so slowly?" replied the third girl, who had brown hair and was around the same height as the purple-haired girl.

Noi watched the girls bicker in front of him, utterly fascinated. He had very little experience interacting with girls.

"Do you know where the nearest inn is?" asked the tall girl.

Noi nodded, at first unable to speak.

"Do you want me to take you there?" he finally managed.

"Please do, before I die in the street," said the purple haired girl.

"By the way, my name is Hikari," said the brown haired girl. "The lazy one is Kerry and her sister is Rhianna."

Noi introduced himself and led the girls through the streets of Alburn to the inn. Apart from the slight drop in temperature, the city wasn't very different from Alana, where the girls had come from. The change in weather was to be expected, as Alburn was farther north than Alana. The streets were wide and busy with people making their way home, treading swiftly over the cobbled ground.

They reached the inn, which was a fairly large building. There was a notice pinned to the door and Hikari read it in dismay.

"Closed until further notice."

"What?" cried Rhianna. "Why is it closed?"

Kerry sat down on the street.

"This has turned out to be a rubbish day," she moaned.

"It's not so bad," said Rhianna, "I packed some things in case we ended up sleeping outside."

"How are you so organised?" said Kerry, exasperated. "I wouldn't be surprised if you packed for a yeti invasion, I really wouldn't."

Noi wondered to himself if he should invite the girls to stay at the workshop. He knew the potter wouldn't like it at all, but he couldn't leave three travellers with nowhere to sleep.

"I work at a pottery workshop," he said, "you could stay there for tonight."

Rhianna looked at Noi gratefully.

"Thank you! You're a lifesaver!" cried Rhianna, and she hugged him.

Noi was taken aback. It was the first time he'd ever been hugged. He realised this was also the first time he had ever engaged in an actual conversation with girls.

As promised, Noi took them to the workshop, dreading how the potter would react.

The workshop was tucked away down a side street and was identifiable by the displays of pottery in the window. Noi mentally prepared himself for facing the potter's rage at taking in three strangers. He was barely in the door when the potter started yelling at him.

"How long does it take you to buy some food and a simple sack of clay?" he yelled. "Without clay, we would starve-"

He stopped his rant when he noticed Hikari, Kerry and Rhianna standing in the doorway.

"Girls??" he yelled. "So this is what you've been up to! And three of them? You sure know how to get around..."

"Honestly, sir, it's not what it looks like..." began Noi, but the potter didn't listen.

"I give you food. I let you live in my workshop. And what do you do to repay me? Go out with girls while I slave away making vases!"

Noi was used to the potter's rages, but the girls were scared of him. He really looked like he could snap and start trying to kill them all.

"They're travellers," Noi explained slowly while the potter gradually calmed down. "The inn is closed, so I said they could stay here."

The potter shook his head in exasperation.

"Since when did you decide who stays in this house?" he grunted. "I will allow it. For one night."

Typical behaviour for him, thought Noi. *He overreacts, gets angry, slowly calms down and actually gives me what I ask for in the end.*

"There's a spare room upstairs," said Noi. "Follow me."

He led the girls to a small but comfortable attic room. There weren't any beds, but Rhianna assured him they would be fine with a few blankets on the floor. Kerry wasn't too keen on the idea, but Rhianna stamped on her foot before she got a chance to object.

"We shouldn't need to stay for more than a night," said Rhianna.

Noi asked where they were going, and Hikari told the story about the Kelluas she had told countless times in the past few days.

Noi listened, wide eyed. When he was little, he always wanted to be a hero, destroy monsters and save damsels in distress. It came from reading far too many adventure books while he was supposed to be listening in lessons. Noi realised this could be his one opportunity to leave his boring life as an apprentice.

I want to go with them. I don't really know anything about these strange girls, and I also don't know anything about Kelluas, but going with them sounds far more interesting than failing at pottery, thought Noi. *However, I can't leave without a trace. And I don't know if these girls would be too thrilled with a random guy they just met tagging along with them.*

Noi sighed. Perhaps he wasn't meant to leave Alburn.

He left the girls alone and went down to the kitchen, where he began to cook. He enjoyed cooking. At least it was better than pottery. When he was done he called everyone into the kitchen, where they ate what Noi prepared in clay bowls made by the potter.

He prepared the traditional Alburn dish of chicken stuffed with herbs unique to the surrounding woods. The potter ate without showing any particular reaction to the food, as he always did. The girls thought it was amazing. Even Rhianna and Kerry, who were used to food literally fit for a king, enjoyed it.

"This is really good!" said Kerry, as she finished her food.

Noi glowed with pride. He wasn't used to being complimented.

Maybe... Maybe I could come along with them, if I offered to cook for them. It's worth a try.

He cleared away the bowls and waited until the potter returned to his workshop before talking to the girls.

"So, on this journey..." he said, thinking of how he should word his request. He didn't want to sound too desperate. "Do any of you cook?"

"Up until now we've been relying on inns for food," said Hikari. "I used to cook a bit but I ended up burning everything."

"Kerry and I have never cooked in our lives," said Rhianna, truthfully.

"What will you do if there isn't an inn?" asked Noi. "What if you end up having to sleep outside, far from civilisation?"

I think I ruined my attempt at not sounding desperate.

"And..." Noi paused as he thought of something else he could say. He wasn't used to talking to girls and he was getting stressed out. "What about safety? Surely it isn't safe for three girls to be travelling alone."

Kerry laughed when she realised what he was hinting at.

"Let me guess," she said. "You want to tag along, don't you?"

"Yes, I do want to. I hate it here," Noi replied bluntly.

Noi waited for them to turn him down, but instead he was pleasantly surprised when Hikari said, "We'd love for you to come along! The more people we have, the stronger we'll be when fighting. Also, you're a great cook! But..."

Noi's spirits sank. There had to be a but.

"Can you really leave? These two here both left their homes, but only one of them actually asked permission."

Hikari paused to glare at Kerry.

"The other just left home without telling her parents, and it caused a great scene."

"It doesn't matter," said Noi. "The only person I have is the potter, and to be honest I think he'd be happy to get rid of me. I'm a useless apprentice. I'm sure the potter will be able to get another, more skilled boy to do my job."

There was no regret in his voice.

"If the potter doesn't mind," said Hikari, "we'd love for you to come along."

Noi grinned. He was pretty sure the potter would let him go.

"I won't be able to ask him tonight," said Noi. "If I interrupt him while he's in his workshop, he won't be happy."

Rhianna nodded. The potter's rage scared her.

They called it a night and went back to their room. The moon was bright and the light spilled into the room through the small window in the roof. As usual, Kerry knelt to pray before she slept. Hikari still thought Kerry was wasting her time, but she found herself interested in what she was saying. She listened in as she pretended to be asleep.

"Dear Heavenly Father," she began, like Liza used to. "Thank you for continuing to support and sustain us on this journey. Thank you also for reuniting Rhianna and me, because I know our fighting goes against your design for families. Please give us the strength to defeat the Kelluas so no more children will be killed. I know there are not many of us and we're not very strong, but with your power even a small shepherd boy can rise up to slay a giant."

"And finally, Lord… Please save Hikari! Help her realise the only person who can give her the peace and comfort she truly seeks is your son, Jesus. Please save her and everyone else we meet like you saved me all those years ago."

"In Lord Jesus' name, Amen."

With that she finished and crawled under the blankets. Conflicted, Hikari gazed up at the window as she thought about what Kerry had said. She was surprised to be mentioned, and she felt strangely happy. However, she refused to overthink it. Eventually, she turned over to sleep. Apart from Kerry complaining bitterly about sleeping on the floor, they slept well.

When morning came they woke early and waited patiently for the potter so Noi could ask about going travelling.

They ate breakfast, and at last the potter came into the kitchen. Noi wasted no time.

"Master, I wish to no longer be your apprentice, but instead I would like to accompany these girls on their quest."

The potter was taken aback by such a sudden request. Then he smiled.

"Thank goodness. It's about time I got a new apprentice. I was wondering how I should break the news to you, but it seems I don't have to. I guess the feeling's mutual; neither of us want to work together."

Noi wasn't sure if he should be happy or offended.

The girls, however, were ecstatic.

"Yay! Someone who can cook!" squealed Kerry.

"It's good to have you on board," said Rhianna, and she shook Noi's hand.

"Now we have someone who is good at cooking, someone who is good at navigation, someone who is good at fighting... and... uh..." Kerry struggled to think of something she was good at.

"You're good at... adding comic relief to otherwise serious circumstances," said Hikari.

"So you're basically saying I'm an idiot," laughed Kerry.

"That's exactly what she's saying," said Rhianna with a wink.

"How about you stupidly talented people shut up so we can get a move on?" said Kerry, pretending to be offended.

They went to the door, and Noi said his final goodbyes to the potter.

"Noi," said the potter. "Do me a favour and never use a potter's wheel again."

Noi laughed.

"Next time, try to pick a better apprentice," he retorted.

Noi walked away from the workshop without looking back. A whole new world awaited him.

At last, I'm finally free, he thought, gladly. *Free from orphanages and apprenticeships.*

Chapter 7

The four started to head towards the northern way out of Alburn, when someone ran into Rhianna from behind. She turned round to see a blonde boy around the same age as her. She recognised him right away.

"Yuti!" she said in surprise.

"Is he a friend of yours?" asked Noi, confused as to who this strange blonde guy was.

"Sort of," said Hikari.

Yuti's face was flushed and it looked like he had been running for some time. He was still carrying the axe he had used to fight Kyros in Azure Falls. He had bought new clothes since they had last seen him, replacing the threadbare homemade clothes he wore before with clothes of a much better quality for travelling.

"You have to go back to Azure Falls," Rhianna told Yuti. "Ailsa and her parents are very worried about you."

Yuti shrugged.

"It's not like they're my real family. And anyway, I'm doing this for Ailsa."

"Why not join with us then?" asked Hikari. "If there were five of us, we could take down the Kelluas, no problem."

"Why would I want to ally with some pathetic little girls who think they're so great purely because they have fancy swords?" Yuti replied.

Noi coughed.

"Sorry. Make that three little girls and one guy who has nothing better to do than stalk them," said Yuti.

Noi resisted the urge to punch Yuti. He already severely disliked this person, despite it only being their first meeting.

"Hikari, if this is a friend I don't want to meet your enemies," said Noi.

Hikari turned away from Yuti.

"Fine. If you don't want to help, we can go our separate ways," Hikari said dismissively as she walked off. Noi, Kerry and Rhianna quickly followed.

"Wait!" yelled Yuti. "I didn't even get to tell you what I meant to tell you before you started banging on about returning to Azure Falls."

Hikari reluctantly turned around.

"Make it quick. We want to get on the road."

"That's exactly it," said Yuti. "The northern way out is blocked because of a massive landslide in the mountains."

"What?" cried Kerry. "We need to get to Tura before the Kelluas attack!"

"I know you do."

Yuti smiled for the first time since Kyros nearly kidnapped Ailsa, but it was a cold hearted smile.

"I, however, know how to bypass the landslide and still get to Tura by nightfall. This proves I have far more chance of defeating the Kelluas and you should all give up."

Yuti laughed and ran down the street. The girls and Noi were too shocked to follow him.

Kerry clenched her fists.

"Why does he see this as some kind of competition?" she said angrily. "Does he not realise children's lives are at stake?"

In a way, Yuti is a bit like I was back at the castle. I let my pride get in the way of doing what is right, thought Rhianna.

"I suppose we should see this blockage for ourselves, instead of standing here and getting frustrated," said Noi.

The girls agreed and they walked north through the cobbled streets of the city. There were many children playing in them. When they got to the northern exit, two guards blocked their way. They couldn't see the blockage, but the guards said it was further in. The guards also said the Northern Mountains were very dangerous at that time of year, and avalanches were common. They wouldn't let them pass.

"But we need to get to Tura!" protested Kerry.

"Unless you want to die in an avalanche, I recommend you stay here for now," said the guard dismissively.

***

Meanwhile, Yuti ran through the shady backstreets of Alburn until he found the lady who had promised to get him to Tura by nightfall. She was entirely covered by a large black cloak, but Yuti could tell from her voice she was a girl not much older than he was. She claimed she was a witch who would be able to get him past the blockage as long as he ran some 'errands' for her.

"I met those girls, although I don't know why you're so interested in them. They're going to Tura too," Yuti reported. "Now you have to uphold your end of the deal."

The woman laughed at him.

"Foolish boy. I never expected you to be so thick. My plan is going better than I expected," she said.

She threw off her cloak, and Yuti realised in horror it was Saya, the pink haired Kellua he had fought in Azure Falls.

"Thanks to you, we now know those girls think we are going to Tura, which confirms our suspicions Kyros blabbed. I guess we'll just have to eliminate them here," explained Saya, still laughing.

Yuti had left Azure Falls before he'd had a chance to listen to Kyros' story, so he was very confused. However, it was as clear as day to him that he had been tricked. He raised his axe in anger.

"Ooh, are we going to fight again?" asked Saya, pretending to be scared.

"Last time we fought, you had to run away," Yuti reminded her.

"Yes, but last time you fought me those three girls were fighting alongside you. On your own, you are nothing."

Yuti growled.

"I'll prove you wrong!" he yelled, as he charged at Saya. "I am more powerful than all of them combined!"

Saya swiftly lifted herself off the ground and started hurling pink balls of energy. Yuti tried to defend himself but his axe was too heavy to be used for both defence and offence. He struggled to land any hits while Saya managed to hit Yuti numerous times before he even got close to her. Overwhelmed, he collapsed on the ground, unconscious.

"Is that all you got?" Saya laughed as she landed back on the ground.

Saya hoped defeating Yuti would help redeem herself for her failure on the last mission. The Superior had not been happy when she returned and told him she had been defeated, and she had left Kyros at the scene. Saya was also hopeful the experiment would soon be completed. All she wanted was to come out of hiding and live a normal life. Some personal human slaves would be a nice bonus as well.

I know who my slaves would be, she thought. *Unless they get killed along the way, I want those three pesky girls to tend to my every need. It will serve them right for making me look like a fool in front of the Superior.*

Anyway, I need to bring this obnoxious boy back to the Superior.

I really wish the Superior would tell us his name, she thought as she grabbed Yuti's arm. *Always calling him 'the Superior' is so annoying. At least I managed to succeed this time. The Superior will be pleased to discover I managed to bring him one of the humans who pose a threat to our plan.*

Saya teleported while holding onto Yuti, filling the air with the sound of sinister laughter.

***

Kerry paced around the paved surface of Alburn's town square in frustration. Hikari, Rhianna and Noi were sitting on a bench, feeling defeated.

"The Kelluas could be attacking innocent people, and we're stuck here!" complained Kerry as she continued aimlessly pacing up and down the square. "Rhianna, are you sure there's no way to bypass the blockage?"

"I'm afraid so," said Rhianna solemnly. "The landslide blocks the main path. If we strayed from the main path through the mountains, we would almost certainly get lost. There's also the risk of avalanches. Trying to go through the mountains would be like walking into a death trap."

"Isn't this whole quest a giant death trap?" remarked Kerry. "What if we bypassed the mountains completely? Can we walk around them?"

Rhianna glared at Kerry for asking such a stupid question.

"The Northern Mountains are the largest mountain range on the continent. If we were to walk around them, it could take us weeks."

Kerry groaned.

"It normally takes them a few weeks to clear landslides," said Noi.

It was around midday, and the town square was quiet apart from a few people passing through. Everyone in the town was busy with work, school or something else, and Kerry hated sitting around.

Noi was also very disappointed, but unlike Kerry, he kept quiet. He was beginning to wonder if he was ever going to leave Alburn.

Rhianna looked up and saw a familiar figure enter the square. She jumped to her feet.

"Yuti!"

The others looked up and saw it was indeed Yuti.

Kerry laughed and put her hands on her hips.

"What happened to your plan of bypassing the landslide and reaching Tura before nightfall? Hmm?"

Yuti didn't reply.

This surprised Kerry, who was expecting a sarcastic remark from him. Yuti stood still and did nothing for a while, and then he slowly raised his axe.

"Hey, what are you doing?" she exclaimed. "I know we're not exactly buddies, but is attacking us going to get you anywhere?"

Saya was watching Yuti from the corner of the square as she hid behind a pillar. She grinned. The Superior's plan was working out better than she had expected. Yuti had succumbed to the Superior's magic and was now fully under her control. She knew those annoying humans would never attack someone they knew, even if they didn't particularly like him.

She resisted the urge to laugh, as she didn't want to blow her cover.

I'm enjoying this. Come on, mind slave. Rid us of these parasites.

Yuti came closer to Kerry.

"Yuti, what are you doing?" shouted Rhianna. "We're not your enemy. We weren't the ones who tried to kidnap Ailsa, it was the Kelluas. Take your rage and direct it at them, not us."

Yuti wasn't paying attention to anything. He had a blank expression on his face, and he showed no intention of lowering his axe.

"What do we do? Attack him?" asked Noi, panicking.

"No!" shouted Hikari. "That would make us no better than the Kelluas!"

"Then what do we do?" asked Kerry.

"Run!" cried Hikari, and she took off down the nearest street. The others wasted no time and followed her.

Ugh, what a pain, thought Saya. *I was hoping they would stand their ground and fight. Oh well, Yuti will have to hunt them down.*

Saya gave Yuti the order to give pursuit. Gleefully, she followed along behind him, being careful not to become visible.

This is why I want to defeat the humans. Having them under my control is much, much more fun than hiding from them.

The girls and Noi ran through the streets of Alburn with Yuti following closely behind. Many of the city's inhabitants stared in shock at the sight of four kids being chased by another kid with an axe, while some joined the chase and tried to stop Yuti.

They kept running through the streets, even when it became hard to keep going. Panic gave them an extra boost of energy. The chase eventually consisted of Hikari,

Kerry, Rhianna and Noi at the front, with Yuti behind them. Behind Yuti were several strangers who were trying their best to catch him. Hikari would have laughed at the ridiculousness of it all had she not been preoccupied with running for her life.

Eventually the girls and Noi began to get tired, and so did Yuti.

Saya remembered the Superior warning her that if she played with her new toy too much, it would break. In other words, she wasn't to drive him to the point of exhaustion.

Saya faced a dilemma. If she made Yuti give up the chase, he would be caught by the townspeople behind him, and she would lose her brand new mind slave. If she made him keep running, he would collapse and the townspeople would again be able to catch him.

Oh no, what do I do now? The Superior is going to kill me! This was my last chance!

She decided to order Yuti to turn around and attack the townspeople instead; however he only ran a few metres in their direction before starting to slow down.

Agh! This is so annoying! Why do humans have so little energy?

Saya accepted defeat and abandoned her control over Yuti.

I'm going to get murdered when I go back. I could pull a Kyros, but I think I'd rather die than become human.

Saya teleported back to the Superior, reluctantly ready to report on her latest failure.

Meanwhile, an extremely confused Yuti was being dragged to the mayor of Alburn by several angry townspeople.

The girls and Noi watched in amazement as Yuti was dragged away.

"What… What just happened?" asked Kerry, panting for breath after all that running.

"That insane friend of yours tried to kill us, in broad daylight, in front of many people," said Noi, also panting heavily.

"Where are they taking him?" asked Kerry, with a hint of concern in her voice.

"How can you be concerned about someone who tried to kill you?" asked Noi, exasperated.

"He has family waiting for him to come home," said Kerry sadly. "It doesn't look like he'll be returning anytime soon."

"The way crime and punishment works here is that if the offender is an outsider, he gets thrown out of Alburn and can never return," explained Noi. "It's good for the offender, but it means there'll be an insane axe-wielding maniac on the loose."

Rhianna remembered Yuti's adoptive mother desperately asking them to convince him to come home.

"We need to see the mayor," she said, "and we need to make sure Yuti returns to Azure Falls. I'm sure Ailsa is waiting for him."

We got chased by an insane maniac with an axe, and they want to make sure he gets home safely? thought Noi. *I think he should be locked up in prison. And perhaps these girls should be locked up in an asylum!*

Noi led the girls to the mayor's house.

The mayor's house was near the town square, and it was considerably larger than the other houses. It was three stories high and had large decorated windows. A huge, ornate clock face was displayed on the front of the building.

Noi knocked on the door. A middle age woman opened it, and she looked flustered.

"Could you come back later? We're a bit busy."

"We're… acquaintances of the guy you brought in," Noi said.

"And we'd like to make sure he returns home to his family," continued Rhianna.

"Oh!" said the woman, surprised. "Maybe you could help us then. He's refusing to co-operate."

The girls and Noi went into the house. It was richly decorated on the inside, and there was an ornate fireplace in the centre of the room. The carpet was a rich red colour, not much different than the carpets Rhianna and Kerry were used to back at their castle. Noi had never been in the mayor's house before, and he was fascinated by the grandeur.

"My husband's study is this way," said the woman, leading them up a flight of stairs. "That's where the man is being held."

In the study, Yuti was being questioned by the mayor. However, Yuti had no idea how he got there. He remembered realising the cloaked witch was actually a Kellua, and then everything was murky beyond that point.

The mayor slammed his fists down on his desk.

"Don't try to play the 'crazy Kellua made me do it' card with me, young man! Why were you threatening innocent people with an axe?" the mayor demanded to know for the thousandth time.

"I'm telling you, I didn't do anything of the sort," growled Yuti. "I was passing through town, and I must have collapsed. Then I woke up here, and everyone is accusing me of being an axe murderer. Yes, I have an axe, but this is for fighting monsters as I travel. I have no intention of harming innocent people."

"You might as well save us all time and admit you did it," said the mayor. "Do you think I'm going to believe over twenty eye-witnesses who said you did it, or one traveller who claims to be innocent?"

At that moment, the girls and Noi entered the room.

"Look!" said the mayor. "These are the very people you chased!"

Yuti felt his anger rise.

"You lying little-"

"Yuti, Yuti..." said Rhianna quickly, before he started throwing accusations at her. "We will pretend all this never happened if you go home."

"I'm telling you all, I never did anything!" Yuti screamed in frustration.

Is he being serious? thought Kerry. *Yuti seems to have something against us, but I don't think he would actually want to kill us.*

"Yuti, what is your last memory before waking up here?" asked Kerry, determined to get to the bottom of why Yuti didn't remember chasing them.

Yuti's eyes widened with sudden recognition.

"Yes! It must have been her!" he shouted, jumping to his feet. "Her, the pink haired Kellua. Talking to her is my last memory! She must be behind this!"

I knew it. This whole situation stinks of Kellua involvement, thought Kerry.

"Saya!" shouted Rhianna. "I knew Kelluas had strange powers, but do you think they can control humans as well? It could be part of the experiment Kyros was telling us about."

"I don't know," said Yuti, frustrated. "I can't remember anything."

"Saya must have brainwashed you," said Kerry, angrily. "Go home, Yuti," said Hikari, rather testily. "You wanted to stop the Kelluas, but instead you ended up helping one."

"And what if I don't go home?" asked Yuti angrily.

The mayor, who had been silent up to this point, coughed.

"I don't know what you are all babbling about, but I would like to point out that if the offender doesn't get out of Alburn soon we will have to throw him out. He's officially banned from staying here, and the path north will be blocked for some time."

"Yuti!" called Rhianna, in a serious tone. "If you're so opposed to going back to Azure Falls, why not join us? I know we've said this many times, but if you act solo you're only going to get into trouble. Look at what happened today."

Yuti stood up angrily.

"You know what? Fine," Yuti said as he threw his axe on the floor. The mayor was horrified at the dent it made on the polished wood.

"I'll go home. You girls can play hero, I don't care. I'd rather go back home than be seen with the likes of you."

Yuti got up and walked to the door without looking back.

The mayor was extremely confused as to what was happening.

"I have no idea what any of you are on about, but thank you for getting that criminal out of this city. I was beginning to think I'd need to force him out."

This town has the strangest justice system, thought Rhianna. *I remember learning about it. Their way of dealing with criminals is to simply banish them from Alburn. After that, they become someone else's problem.*

They left the mayor's house and sat in the town square again. They couldn't help but feel sorry for Yuti. If not for his pride, he might have been a valuable asset in the fight against the Kelluas.

At least Ailsa and her parents would be able to see him again.

"What do we do now?" said Kerry, asking the obvious question.

"I really don't know," Rhianna said, "We should probably stay clear of Azure Falls. Yuti hates us."

Kerry moaned.

"We have no idea about anything..." she complained.

"First you moan about having to walk too much. Now you moan about having nowhere to walk. Seriously, there's no pleasing you," said Rhianna, laughing.

***

Saya waited fearfully for the Superior to arrive. Michius was also in the room, grinning to himself. He brushed a strand of his messy hair out of his face.

"You know, I've never seen you so quiet," he sneered.

"Shut up!" she snapped in reply.

The Superior entered the room.

He had jet black hair that fell all over his face, and his cloak was a similar colour. He wore a hat that cast a shadow over his face and in the dim light of the cave Saya couldn't see his facial expression at all.

"I hear you've failed me," he said in a very deep voice.

"I did," said Saya, meekly.

Normally Saya would put up a huge argument if anyone dared to criticise her, but she was too scared of what the Superior might do to her.

"Why did you fail?" asked the Superior, his voice surprisingly calm.

"My mind slave became unstable."

"Why didn't you attack the humans directly then?"

Saya flinched. She had been dreading that question.

"I... I thought it would be unwise to fight on my own," she stuttered.

"In other words, you ran away like a coward," said the Superior, his tone changing from calm to extremely angry.

"But sir!" Saya protested. "Just two of those humans managed to defeat Kyros and Michius on the island. How could I defeat four of them on my own?"

"If you had at least tried, and then retreated like you did last time, I wouldn't be so annoyed," said the Superior. "However, you left without a fight."

Saya hung her head.

"Hey, at least she got that kid with the axe to get off our trail. I doubt he'll want to mess with us again after that incident," said Michius, who surprised even himself by defending Saya.

The Superior was silent as he wondered if he should punish Saya or not.

"You have one more chance," he declared. "Fail one more time, and I won't be so forgiving."

He left without saying another word.

Michius laughed.

"You owe me one now, you know," he said.

Saya clenched her fists. She really, really hated the Superior.

Chapter 8

Michius and Oden were put in charge of the next mission. The Superior had decided to postpone his goal of kidnapping a child, and he told Michius and Oden to concentrate on killing Hikari, Kerry, Rhianna and Noi. He was extremely frustrated that a bunch of kids had thwarted his plans more than once.

Saya was currently back in Alburn, trying to redeem herself. Her orders were to stay hidden and survey the humans in the city, to find out if news of the Kelluas' return had reached human ears. Michius was waiting for Saya to return, so he could base his plan on her report. Oden was nowhere to be seen, but that didn't surprise him. Oden was mysterious, and he often came and went from the Kellua hideout as much as he wanted, which annoyed the Superior.

Just as Michius was thinking about him, Oden entered the room. His shoulder length green hair was wet from rain.

"The Superior will be thrilled when he hears you've been outside again," said Michius, not really caring.

"I don't mind," replied Oden. "He can't expect us to wait in here until we get a mission. I understand he doesn't want us to blow our cover, but we're basically prisoners. Doesn't that bother you?"

"Not really. Before the Superior gathered us together, I spent my life in hiding from the humans. Not much different from what I'm doing now," said Michius.

"It may suit you fine, but I hate it," said Oden with a sneer. "Why can't Saya hurry up so we can get on with our mission?"

They hung around in the gloomy room, waiting for Saya. Michius suggested a game of cards with a pack he had recently stolen from a pub in a human town, but Oden refused. The atmosphere was always awkward between the Kelluas. None of them particularly liked each other.

Eventually Saya returned, looking depressed.

"How are things?" asked Oden, itching to hear what she had to say.

"Worse than we thought," she said solemnly. "Reports from people who saw us in Azure Falls have reached Alburn, and people are starting to realise we actually exist. It's only a matter of time before people realize the threat we represent and decide to take action."

"So, you and Kyros really blew our cover then," said Oden grimly.

"I'm surprised the Superior hasn't killed you yet. You've certainly failed a lot," said Michius.

Saya resisted the urge to start attacking Michius and Oden. Out of all the Kelluas, she was the most uncomfortable with the current situation. As the only female Kellua left, it always weighed on her mind that if they really did defeat the humans the Superior would probably want them to start repopulating.

"At least I didn't run away like Kyros," she growled as she left the room.

Oden turned to Michius.

"So, what's the plan?" he asked.

Michius thought for a moment.

"We know all attempts to dispose of the young humans by direct confrontation have failed," he said, deep in thought. "We also have to remember one more person has joined them. Currently he is unarmed, but I still wouldn't overlook him."

"On top of that, many other humans are now aware of our existence. If they saw us, they would be likely to attack us," said Oden. "It seems like our only chance of eliminating our assailants is by attacking from afar. Our powers are still too weak for frontal assaults."

Silence filled the room as both Kelluas tried to think of how they could attack from a distance, preferably without being noticed. When Michius was about to give up, Oden suddenly grinned.

"I've got it," he said excitedly. "An explosion. We'll blow them up."

"And how exactly will we do that?" asked Michius, thinking practically. "We don't have a power that lets us explode things."

"Gunpowder, and lots of it," said Oden, excitedly. "We place it during the night so no-one sees us, then we throw an energy ball at it and teleport to a safe distance away before it ignites."

"That might work," admitted Michius, who was annoyed that Oden thought of a good plan before he did. "However, where will we get the amount of gunpowder required?"

"We'll steal it from somewhere," explained Oden. "It shouldn't be a problem."

"Let's go and get ourselves some gunpowder, then," said Michius.

***

Michius and Oden travelled to Alana Castle, Kerry and Rhianna's home, because they'd heard there was a large supply of gunpowder in the basement for defence purposes. However, the supplies were heavily guarded. They decided the easiest course of action would be to knock the guards out and then teleport the gunpowder away as quickly as they could.

"Hey! Unauthorised personnel aren't allowed down here!" yelled one of the guards when he saw the two Kelluas enter the basement.

"Wait…" said another guard as he started backing away. "You're… those things that destroyed the village on the island!"

Oden sighed.

"That's come out already? I guess our cover is well and truly blown," he said. "That means it won't matter if I do THIS!"

He floated a few centimetres of the ground and started throwing green energy balls. The guards were completely unprepared for an attack of the supernatural kind, and they floundered as they bore Oden's attacks. Michius quickly did the same, and soon all the guards were lying on the floor, unconscious. The fight had barely begun before it was over. The Kelluas didn't want to take any chances, so they had decided to kill any humans they met.

Oden grabbed a barrel and lifted it up. Michius did the same.

Suddenly, someone ran down the basement steps. They were light footed and they barely made a sound. In fact, they were so quiet Michius didn't even notice their presence until it was too late. The girl swung a sword at the back of his head and he died before he knew what had hit him. The barrel he had been holding fell to the ground with a crash and the contents spilled all over the floor.

Oden turned around in shock and saw a girl standing before him with a grimace on her face and a huge sword in her hands. She didn't look much older than twelve, and she was dressed in a black and white dress. Pinned to her chest was a badge that read 'Kamitika – castle librarian' in gold lettering.

"Anyone who tries to attack this castle has to come through me!" she yelled, before charging at Oden with her sword, which she had taken from the castle armoury.

After Rhianna and Kerry left the castle with Hikari, Kamitika had read every single page of the book on Kelluas. She knew how to fight them. Since Kerry's most recent departure, Kamitika had continued diligently carrying out her duties in the library. However, her concern for her old friend grew significantly, especially when rumours started spreading around Alana that both princesses had been sighted fighting Kelluas.

After hearing the crash in the basement, she panicked and grabbed a sword. At first, she was shocked to see actual Kelluas were in the castle. However, when she saw the guards lying on the ground, she instinctively when into attack mode.

Next, Kamitika clashed with Oden. She had never fought properly before, but her strong sense of righteous indignation fuelled her on. She had to make sure he didn't ignite the gunpowder. Oden soon tired, and he found himself wondering if he should continue fighting in the hope of killing Kamitika, or retreat back to base. If he died, the only Kelluas left would be the Superior and Saya. He knew those two could never reclaim the lost land on their own.

It was this thought that convinced Oden to stop fighting. He teleported away and left Kamitika standing on her own, trembling with the realisation she'd actually killed a monster and scared off another.

Kamitika looked at the carnage around her. Many barrels of gunpowder had been broken and black powder covered the floor. Michius' body lay in the corner. More palace guards ran into the basement and saw the state of the room.

They saw the sword in Kamitika's hands, and they were shocked the twelve year old librarian was such a mighty warrior.

Kamitika turned to one of them.

"One got away," she said. "Spread the word around the continent that there are dangerous Kelluas on the loose, attacking people."

The guards nodded and ran to tell the King and Queen what had happened.

Please Kerry, Rhianna, Hikari... thought Kamitika. *Wherever you are, please be safe...*

Chapter 9

Kerry, Rhianna, Hikari and Noi were stuck in Alburn for nearly a week, waiting for the path north to be cleared, but unfortunately clearing the blockage was taking longer than anticipated.

They filled time by hanging around the town square and practicing sparring with each other. Rhianna had bought Noi a weapon similar to hers, but to his embarrassment all three of the girls could beat him within a minute.

"It's OK," Rhianna assured him. "You'll get better over time."

"And if that fails, you can hide behind a rock while we fight the Kelluas," laughed Kerry.

Noi was used to this sort of teasing from Kerry and Hikari. The girls were so bored hanging around in the Alburn inn that they started playing various pranks on the only male member of their group. This included convincing him the inn was haunted and putting ribbons in his hair while he slept. He was particularly annoyed over the last one, because he walked about Alburn all day before noticing the ribbons. Rhianna didn't take part in the pranks Kerry and Rhianna liked to pull, but she secretly thought they were pretty funny. Noi, however, had managed to get his own back by dousing their food in chili pepper. The chaos that ensued was well worth the ribbons.

Kerry put down her sword and sat on a bench.

"Why can't they clear the path faster?" she moaned. "I'd rather go on a wild goose chase than no chase at all."

They heard a horse approaching and Rhianna and Kerry instantly recognised the Alana castle uniform the rider was wearing. The horse stopped and he dismounted.

"Princesses!" he shouted as he hastily bowed. "I bring news from Alana."

"Has something bad happened?" asked Rhianna, worried.

"Those things that you were sighted fighting in Azure Falls... Kelsomethings... they were in the castle a few days ago!"

Kerry gasped.

"Kelluas! Was anyone hurt?"

The messenger nodded solemnly.

"Two guards were injured," he recalled. "There were two Kelluas, and they broke into the basement to steal gunpowder."

"There were two of them?" asked Hikari. "What did they look like?"

"According to Kamitika, one had blue hair and the other had green hair," replied the messenger.

"Kamitika?" asked Kerry, shocked. "Is she OK?"

"She went down to the basement and killed the blue haired Kellua. She then started to fight with the other one, but it got away."

Kamitika? Fighting? thought Kerry, amazed.

"Also, the King and Queen are very displeased with both of you," said the messenger. "You told them that your companion was a travelling merchant, but instead the both of you have been sighted fighting dangerous creatures."

"They're going to kill me..." Kerry muttered.

"The King and Queen ordered me to bring both of you back to the castle," said the messenger.

No! thought Kerry. *After all this, I'm not going back. Perhaps I'll return someday, but not now. I want to defeat the Kelluas.*

"The Queen is very concerned for your safety," explained the messenger. "Not only are you fighting monsters, the news that you were chased through the streets of this city by a dangerous man spread fast. The King is also worried about the impact it's having on Alana's reputation. What kind of kingdom lets its princesses abandon their duty to fight dangerous monsters?"

"We're not going back, and you can't make us," snapped Rhianna, firmly. "Tell mother and father we will return once our quest is complete. We will do our best not to get killed, but if we fall in battle it's a necessary and noble sacrifice. These creatures must be stopped."

Impressed by their courage, the messenger nodded and he decided to stop arguing.

"Fine then," said the messenger. "I'll report back to the castle. When they hear the news, your parents may send more people out to bring you home. I cannot lie to them, but I will purposely take the long route back to buy you as much time as possible."

"Thank you!" said Kerry, and she hugged the messenger.

He bowed and left the square.

"This is bad," said Rhianna, "now mother and father are on to us."

"And they know where we are at the moment," said Kerry. "That messenger was able to find us."

"They probably heard you got chased by an insane axe wielding guy," said Hikari.

Hikari couldn't stop herself from laughing.

"What's so funny?" asked Kerry, annoyed.

"It's just… a few days ago our biggest concern was a tribe of extremely dangerous creatures. Now our biggest concern is your parents tracking us," explained Hikari.

Noi started laughing as well.

"Stop it!" yelled Kerry, but Hikari and Noi found the whole situation hilarious. Then Rhianna started to laugh as well.

Kerry stamped her foot in frustration.

"Glad to know you're so concerned, Rhianna," she huffed.

"Come on Kerry, think about it," said Rhianna. "The worst that could happen is we go home. Hikari and Noi should be able to handle it. However, it's important that they act fast. The Kelluas are only weak because they don't yet have their full powers."

"But I don't want to go home!" shouted Kerry, behaving like a toddler having a tantrum. "Home is the boringest place on Maysea! It's all study, study, study…"

"Deal with it, Princess Kerry," said Noi, still laughing. "Also, boringest isn't a word."

"That's it!" shouted Kerry, and she tackled Noi to the ground. She cringed at the use of her proper title.

"Hey! Get off me!" shouted Noi.

Several townspeople were staring at them as they struggled on the ground.

"Kerry, you're so immature," said Hikari, sighing.

Rhianna dragged Kerry off Noi.

"Let's try not to kill each other, OK?" said Rhianna.

Kerry pulled a face at Noi as he stood up.

"Rather than continue to mess around, should we check if the blockage is cleared yet?" asked Noi, as he dusted himself down.

"Yeah, that would give us something to do," said Hikari, and they set off to the northern exit of the city.

Checking the exit had become somewhat of a daily ritual, with the same disappointing result each time.

Yesterday, they had been told it wouldn't be long until the path was open again, so Hikari was hopeful it would be open this time.

In the last few days they had been preparing for their walk through the mountains by buying lots of food and getting Noi warm clothes (he refused to wear anything belonging to Rhianna or Kerry).

Upon reaching the site of the blockage, they were relieved to see it had been cleared.

"Yay!" shouted Kerry. "We can finally leave this place!"

She ran down the path and the others quickly followed. At last, they could resume their quest.

***

Saya, Oden and the Superior were sitting around a table, talking in the dim light of their hideout. The Superior was not pleased. Morale was extremely low amongst the Kelluas, with their numbers steadily decreasing and the experiment looking less likely to reach completion with each passing day.

"Our numbers have been reduced to three," he said, sternly. "If things continue like this, we will become extinct. We have underestimated the strength of these human girls."

"But they're not our only enemies," Saya pointed out. "Michius was killed by another human."

"I know," said the Superior. "We must still be cautious, and remain out of sight when possible. Until we regain our full strength, we remain extremely vulnerable to attack."

"What's our next plan?" asked Oden.

"We will attack Tura as we originally planned," said the Superior. "Those meddlesome children know we plan to go there, but with our teleportation we should beat them to it."

"There's also a possibility news of our return hasn't reached so far north yet," said Saya. "The same can't be said for towns closer to Alana. We have to assume the humans there have been alerted to our presence and are postured to defend against us. Trying to nab a child from one of those towns would be extremely risky."

The Superior nodded and stood up.

"This is our next plan: the two of you will go to Tura. See if there are any children living there, and if there are, seize them so we can conduct our experiment. I'll let you decide the method, but remember that I will not tolerate cowardice. Understood?"

"Yes sir!" chimed Saya and Oden.

What I want to know is why the Superior himself doesn't go on any missions, thought Saya. *What does he even do all day?*

She knew better than to ask such a question.

Obeying their master's command, Saya and Oden teleported out of the hideout and headed for Tura.

***

Meanwhile, Hikari, Kerry, Rhianna and Noi made their way towards Tura. Tura was situated in the foothills of the Northern Mountains. The temperature steadily decreased as they approached the mountains. Before long, they were each wearing heavy coats, and even then they could still see their breaths lingering with each exhalation. Their hands were cold and the wind bit at their faces as they trudged on.

The mountains towered over their heads and gave them all a sense of foreboding. The jagged outcrops of rock that surrounded them made the landscape look inhospitable and uninviting.

Rhianna was walking ahead with Noi, and Kerry and Hikari were lagging behind.

"Hey, Hikari," said Kerry. "What are you planning on doing when all this is over?"

Kerry had been meaning to ask Hikari that question for some time.

"I really don't know," Hikari admitted. "All I care about now is avenging Liza's death."

"I was wondering…." Kerry wondered how she should phrase her next question. "Do you ever pray about things?"

"Not really," said Hikari.

I don't think I've said a single prayer since my parents died, thought Hikari. *I remember Liza used to always pray before going to bed. I never did. I was too busy taking care of Liza to talk to someone who probably doesn't even exist.*

Hikari was reminded of the night she heard Kerry pray for her, and the strange emotions she felt.

"Oh," said Kerry, trying to be casual. "Well, perhaps you should try it some time."

"I've never really been into the whole religion thing," said Hikari dismissively. "I prefer to live my life without over-thinking the philosophy of everything."

"This isn't some boring religion though. Christianity is totally different!" Kerry pushed. "You're not worshipping some lame idol and you can have an awesome relationship with God himself through his son, Jesus. He actually answers when you talk to him. Not through words, but through other mysterious ways."

"Let me guess, you're going to tell me he died for my sins and I need to be 'saved'," Hikari replied with a snort.

"Believe me, I got the same spiel from my family almost daily. Look Kerry, I appreciate the fact you care about my spiritual well-being. But I don't believe in God, plain and simple. I certainly don't believe he died for me on some mythical mother world called Earth, which probably doesn't exist either. There's just us, and we're all alone."

Kerry detected the sadness in her voice. Hikari truly believed she was alone. With the loss of her family she had been left to feel there wasn't anyone in the whole universe left to care for her. Kerry wanted to change that.

"But don't you ever think there's more to life beyond your personal bubble?" asked Kerry. "How do you explain the awesomeness of everything? The stunning sunrise, the gorgeous trees, the majestic animals... Hikari, the proof of God's existence is all around you! Do you really think all of this is an accident?"

How come she's suddenly gone all poetic on me? I never imagined Kerry as the sentimental type.

"I have a question for you, then," said Hikari. "How do you explain suffering? How come my village was destroyed? Why is my entire family dead? Do you call that the awesomeness of everything?"

Kerry wasn't sure how to reply to this.

"There are things we simply can't explain," Kerry said quietly. She knew it was a weak response. "God has a plan for all of us, and sometimes it can seem bad to us. We don't have a divine look at things to put the big picture into perspective."

"I don't want to put my trust in something you can't even explain properly to me," said Hikari with a sneer.

They walked on in silence.

Kerry was annoyed at herself for not explaining things better.

Oh well, she thought. *I'll try again another time. I won't give up. What was it my annoying old tutor used to say? 'Perseverance is the key'. When he said it he was referring to mathematical equations, but I can apply it to this situation as well.*

They walked down the road for hours before finally reaching the village of Tura. Their timing was good, because it started to snow as they arrived. It started off as a few flakes, but by the time they reached the front door of the inn the flakes had turned into a full on blizzard. They could barely make out the village, because everything was covered in a white blanket of snow. They went inside the inn and stamped their feet on the mat to get rid of all the snow on their shoes.

Compared to the other inns they had visited, this one was quite busy. Many travellers stopped there on their way across the Northern Mountains. In better weather the mountains were used as hunting grounds, apparent from the various animal heads decorating the walls. A fire was burning at the corner of the room and several people had hung damp clothes and equipment in front of it to dry.

An old woman sat behind a wooden desk, and the girls and Noi paid for four beds for the night. Their room was simple, but much appreciated after walking in cold temperatures all day.

While lying in bed, Hikari reflected on her talk with Kerry and their disagreement over religion. This got her thinking about Liza's devotion to prayer. Hikari continued thinking of her sister as she drifted off to sleep, and then she began to dream.

***

It was different from her last dream. Instead of watching herself from afar, she was actually in the dream.

She was in the familiar setting of her house in Honif, and she could see three people in the room, one lying in a bed and the other two sitting beside them.

The one in the bed was Hikari's mother. Sitting beside her was Mrs Firr, holding a three year old Liza in her lap.

Hikari was seeing one of her worst memories.

This is worse than last time. Much worse. Why do I have to watch this again! I don't want to!

At the time the memory took place, Hikari was only thirteen. Her father had recently died of an unknown disease, and her mother was also slowly dying.

While Mrs Firr and Liza sat next to her, Hikari sat in the corner of the room, trying to remove herself from what was happening.

I remember this day vividly. How could I ever forget? Everyone was being so kind to me, but I ignored everyone. I refused to eat as well. I wanted to curl up in a ball and forget everything.

Even when she was dying, mother kept praising and praying. I will never understand why she bothered to keep her faith when everything was falling apart. A lot of good it did her in the end.

***

Hikari woke up from her dream with a jolt. Her eyes were wet with tears and she struggled to get back to sleep again.

Kerry was also still awake, but for a different reason. She was praying.

Kerry knew Hikari wasn't instantly going to give her life to Jesus after one conversation, but she couldn't help being sad at Hikari's obvious lack of interest. Kerry felt if Hikari accepted Christ into her heart and believed in the gift of eternal life granted by God to all those who believed in Jesus as their Lord and Saviour, it would help Hikari cope with her sister's death. She loved her friend and she did not want Hikari to continue mourning like those who have no hope.

Both Kerry and Rhianna had attended the church in Alana Castle, but Kerry spent the most time in it. When she was younger she had gone to the church to hide from lessons, and during that time she had spoken to the minister about many things. Kerry couldn't really think of a definite moment when she became a Christian. For as long as she could remember, she had always accepted that God existed, and she trusted in Jesus as her saviour. Of course, she knew she hadn't always been a good child, and she regularly shirked her Bible reading. However, each time she fell away from the Church, she was brought back stronger than before. She had been meaning to ask Rhianna about her beliefs sooner, but there had never been an appropriate time. Also, even though she felt ashamed to admit it, Kerry felt embarrassed when talking to others about her faith. She was worried she would turn them away rather than convince them to believe.

In Alana, Kerry had accepted everyone was Christian until she met Kamitika. To Kamitika church was something you did on Sunday because you had to go. Kerry had tried her best to get Kamitika to attend the church in the castle and, although it was a little awkward at first, Kamitika soon became a regular church goer. In the months after her mother's death, Kamitika had often turned to scriptures for reassurance. She said the idea of her mother having eternal life in heaven greatly comforted her.

Kerry wanted Hikari to think like that. Currently, Hikari's only goal was defeating the Kelluas. But after her goal was achieved, Hikari would literally have nothing left.

No reason to live. Kerry was determined to give her friend a sense of purpose and a reason to live for something other than fuelling her thirst for vengeance.

When morning came the girls and Noi assembled in the front room of the inn. The room was filled with the chatter of many travellers and adventure seekers preparing to scale the Northern Mountains.

The snow was still falling, and a sheet of white obscured the view out of the windows.

"I think we should wait until the blizzard passes before setting out," said Rhianna as she gazed out of the window. "We're not equipped to deal with snow so heavy."

"Suits me," said Kerry, who was lying in a soft chair with her feet on a table. In her hands she had a mug of hot tea she took sips from.

Kerry, Hikari and Rhianna had never seen snow, but Noi had. It snowed for a few days every winter in Alburn, and Noi and his friends in the orphanage had had great fun ambushing monks with snowballs. As for the girls, the only time they had seen snow was in picture books they read when they were children. Kerry was expecting snow to be something magical, like a fluffy white blanket covering the land. She was disappointed to find it was merely a colder version of rain.

* * *

Meanwhile, Saya and Oden were walking around the mountain foothills, struggling to find shelter from the relentless blizzard. Their cloaks were not designed for the weather conditions of the Northern Mountains, and they were both freezing.

We can't possibly attack in conditions like this, Saya thought. *I can't function when I'm this cold! By the time this weather clears, those annoying kids will probably have caught up with us. So much for teleporting.*

They weren't sure if the people living in Tura would recognise them or not, so they couldn't risk seeking shelter in the village.

"I'm so cold!" yelled Saya, gritting her teeth.

"Moaning isn't going to get you anywhere," said Oden, who was sick of Saya's constant grumbling.

"Why did the Superior send us here? Why can't we visit an oasis town or something?" said Saya, continuing to moan.

Oden resisted the urge to slap Saya.

"Who knows what goes on in the Superior's head," replied Oden. "Just shut up and find shelter before we both die."

They trudged through the snow until at last they found a cave that was big enough to sleep in. They settled down and tried to preserve as much warmth as they could.

"Well this sucks," said Saya, blowing on her fingers in an attempt to restore some feeling to them.

"I don't know what's worse," said Oden, "being out in that blizzard, or being stuck in here with you."

"I wish you'd died instead of Michius," hissed Saya in response. "To be honest, I don't really like any of you."

"The feeling's mutual, none of us like you either," retaliated Oden.

It was true. Oden and Michius both thought (or used to think, in Michius' case) Saya was annoying, the Superior thought she was a useless failure and Kyros was terrified of her.

"I bet you're the next to die," said Oden.

"Not if I kill you first," growled Saya.

When the blizzard finally cleared the following morning the Kelluas were relieved.

After a light breakfast of tasteless rations, Saya and Oden used their time in the cave to formulate a plan of action. They would go into the village and they would see if there were any small children they could capture to take back to the hideout. If there were no kids, they would report back to the hideout empty handed and ask the Superior for another town to target. Hopefully someplace much warmer.

Saya stamped her foot on the ground in frustration. She was sore all over after a restless night in the freezing cold.

"I hate this darn experiment!" she yelled.

"Shut up!" snapped Oden. "You'll attract attention to us. We'll have to come up with a new approach."

"Destruction?" asked Saya.

"That's failed every time in the past," said Oden. "We could always try negotiating."

"And how would we do that?" asked Saya, sceptically.

"We'll go into the village and show off our power by smashing some stuff, but we won't harm anyone," explained Oden. "When we've generated enough attention, we'll demand they bring the youngest person in the village to us, or people will get hurt."

"I suppose that could work," said Saya, although she hated agreeing with anything Oden said. "Humans can be pretty selfish. They'll do anything to save their own skin."

"Shall we get on with it then?" asked Oden, taking Saya's hand.

She broke free of his hand in disgust.

"Let's go," she said, and they started walking towards Tura.

Meanwhile, Hikari, Kerry, Rhianna and Noi were ready to leave Tura and they had put on at least three extra layers to fight the cold. Kerry wasn't looking forward to going back out into the snow, and she hoped there wouldn't be another blizzard.

They had just stepped outside when they heard a crash and the sound of people screaming. They looked in the direction of the explosion and their eyes were greeted with the all too familiar sight of Kelluas shooting energy balls. However, this time they didn't seem to be aiming to kill. Instead they were shooting plants, barrels and other inanimate objects.

"What are they playing at?" asked Kerry, confused.

The Kelluas stopped attacking.

"Alright, you humans!" shouted Oden. "Give us the youngest person in this sorry excuse for a village, and no-one gets hurt."

"We'd never do that!" screamed a woman from the back of the crowd that had gathered around Oden. "We know who you are! You're the monsters who broke into Alana Castle!"

"So you know who we are," said Saya, calmly. "Then you must also know how powerful we are. I advise you to do what I say, if you know what's good for you."

Kerry grinned.

"You say you're so powerful, but from what I heard, you were defeated by a twelve year old girl."

Oden and Saya gasped when they saw who spoke.

"Y... you!" Saya stuttered, pointing at Kerry. "All of you!"

Oden laughed bitterly, doing his best to project confidence.

"So you are here after all," he said. "It seems we can't get rid of you kids."

"Don't call us kids!" Rhianna yelled, drawing her sword. The others followed suit.

"We're not letting you get away unscathed," Hikari hissed.

The Superior's orders to not be cowards Saya's mind. This was a battle they couldn't avoid.

If we leave, the Superior will be furious with us. After the amount of times I've messed up, he may even kill me. However, it's four of them against two of us, and there are also these villagers. I bet some of them can fight. What do we do?

Saya looked at Oden, who was also debating his options.

"Let's fight," he whispered to Saya, "but teleport away at the first sign of danger."

Saya nodded.

"We accept your challenge," Saya announced.

"Fine by us," said Kerry, weapon poised.

As Saya had feared, several of the villagers also had weapons and appeared ready to use them. They didn't have expensive weapons like the girls and Noi, but they did have objects such as fire tongs, sticks and rocks, which could still be deadly to the Kelluas if they were hit on the head.

Saya and Oden started to shoot coloured energy balls into the crowd, while trying their best to avoid the rocks being thrown at them.

Hikari got close enough to strike Saya with her scythe, but Saya quickly jumped backwards. She was surrounded by a crowd of angry villagers who continued to throw objects at her from all sides. The best she could do was to use her hands to protect the back of her head. Oden was having similar difficulties with facing such a large crowd. Saya had a sinking feeling they had already lost the battle.

"Let's retreat!" Oden yelled at Saya, over the angry voices of the villagers.

"Yes! Retreat!" cried a man from the crowd, who had been throwing rocks at Saya and Oden. "And tell whoever you are working for that we humans aren't going down without a fight! We know who you are, and all across the continent the news is spreading. Wherever you go, you will be met with defiance. You will never take our children!"

The villagers cheered in agreement.

"I hate humans…" grumbled Saya as she teleported away with Oden.

Saya was genuinely shocked at how the humans had reacted. Her opinion of humans was that they were selfish oppressors. She was convinced they would hand over a child to save themselves, but instead they had risked harming themselves for another. This self-sacrificing attitude was new to Saya.

They'd made a mess of the village, but no-one had been harmed. Many villagers crowded around the girls and Noi, treating them like heroes.

"Are those swords real?" a young boy asked in amazement.

"Yup, they certainly are," replied Kerry, who was enjoying the attention. "They'd better be, we paid a lot for then."

The boy looked at them with pure admiration in his eyes, and Noi was reminded of the way some of the younger boys in the orphanage would look at him after he dared break one of the rules. Noi wished his friends from the orphanage could see him now.

An old man dressed in furs, who was the village elder, made his way through the crowd.

"On behalf of everyone in Tura, I wish to thank you for defending us from those creatures," he said gratefully. He shook their hands in turn.

"It was our pleasure," replied Rhianna.

"Noi still needs to work on his sword skills, though," said Kerry with a smile. In response, Noi threw a handful of snow in her face.

She screamed as it melted and ran down her front.

"I'm going to get you, Noi!" she yelled, as she started to pelt him with snow. Rhianna and Hikari joined in, and soon the entire village had joined in a massive snowball fight.

I'm so glad I met these girls, thought Noi, *even if they are a bit unpredictable at times.*

***

Back at the Kellua hideout, the mood was far from improved. The Superior was furious at Saya and Oden for adding to their long list of consecutive failures.

"Saya, you have failed me too many times. I cannot overlook it anymore."

"Please, Sir…" she started to beg. "Please give me another chance. I'll prove I'm useful!"

"Enough!" yelled the Superior. "The fact is you have not aided our cause in any meaningful way. I should kill you now. However, you are still needed due to our depleted numbers. Even if you are useless at combat."

He then turned to Oden.

"You were never very dedicated to the cause, Oden. Again and again, I've caught you sneaking out, jeopardizing the safety and security of this hideout and our mission with your recklessness. You've also failed your past two assignments. You have ran out of chances."

He raised his arm and began shooting at Oden. Oden grimaced and tried to avoid getting hit, but the Superior was too powerful. None of the Kelluas had actually seen him fight before, and Saya began to get an idea of his true power. The Superior kicked Oden to the ground as Saya looked on, powerless. He shot at the back of Oden's head multiple times to ensure he was dead. Then he revealed a twisted smile and turned his attention to Saya. She dropped to her knees in fear.

"So you're the only one left then," he said. "I think I've learned my lesson. Sending any of you out on missions is pointless. You are all useless as combatants."

"Why didn't you realise that sooner!" yelled Saya, getting back on her feet. "Why wait until three of us are gone?"

"I didn't need them anyway," replied the Superior, calmly. "You're the only one I really need to spawn the next generation of Kellua."

"Why don't you kill me?" Saya yelled. "I'm not going to be used for breeding stock, especially not by the likes of you!"

"You will do as I say," he replied sternly. "If you disobey me I can do much worse than simply kill you. Now, back to the matter at hand. I'm going to take the task of eliminating those pesky human children into my own hands. However, I need you as bait, my darling."

He stroked Saya's face and she quickly slapped his hand away.

"Bait? Is that all I am now?"

Saya felt sick. She wished she'd never gotten herself involved with this sadistic monster. She now realised her own personal safety was much more important than restoring the Kellua to their former position of glory. A new Kellua nation led by the Superior was not worth restoring.

"In order to carry out what I have planned, they need to pass through the Northern Mountains. It's your job to make sure they head in that direction," the Superior explained. "Also, don't let on that Oden is dead. We don't want to give them too much confidence."

"I will, on one condition," Saya said.

"And what would that be?"

"Tell me your name," demanded Saya. "I refuse to call you Superior, because I do not believe you are superior to me in any way."

"Is that all?" he scoffed, as if he had been expecting a more generous request. "I will tell you my name then. It's Corvus. Feel free to call me that, for now. Soon this world will know me as King Corvus!"

"Fine then, Corvus. If that's even your real name," said Saya, rolling her eyes. "What exactly do you want me to do?"

"I don't care what you do, as long as you get those humans to follow you through the Northern Mountains," said Corvus. "Think of something. You know what will happen if you fail."

Saya nodded and grabbed her cloak, the same one she had worn in Alburn to disguise herself. Then she teleported back to the snowfield surrounding Tura. She wasn't sure why she was still obeying Corvus after all he had done to her. She no longer viewed him with reverence as the powerful and mysterious leader she used to think he was. Instead, she saw him as nothing more than a maniac driven mad by an obsession with power. Admittedly, the idea of invincibility and regaining the lands her ancestors had lost still appealed to her, but she was beginning to wonder if it was really worth it. Once Corvus solidified his base of power and used her to repopulate the world with his offspring, it was doubtful he would even have use for her anymore.

Chapter 10

Saya walked through the snow with her teeth chattering, despite her warm cloak. The snow was steadily falling from the sky, and cold water soaked through to her bare skin. As she walked, she wondered how she could coerce Hikari, Rhianna, Kerry and Noi to pass through the Northern Mountains.

I could try starting a rumour, she considered. *Humans can't resist juicy gossip.*

She entered the village and headed straight for the bar, which she thought would be the best place to start a rumour.

The bar was quite crowded, and many travellers were having a drink with the locals. The skins of mountain animals were displayed on the wall, as well as maps of the mountains. There were a few gas lamps, but the room was still quite dim. There was a smoky haze from tobacco pipes that further reduced visibility.

Saya wasn't too keen on alcohol, so she took a seat at one of the tables without ordering anything. It wasn't long before one of the locals sat in the seat next to Saya, and she could tell by the smell of his breath that he had had too much to drink.

"I haven't seen you around these parts before," he said. "You a traveller? You don't get many girls travelling on their own."

"Something like that, yeah," replied Saya.

"Did you just come off the mountains?"

"I spent a few days walking through the mountains."

"You missed some excitement earlier today," said the man while taking a drink from the cup he was holding.

"The village got attacked by these monsters, but some sword wielding girls sent them packing."

Saya began to get interested in the conversation now the topic of the Kelluas had been brought up.

"I recall seeing two suspicious looking individuals on the Northern Mountains, and it looked like they were in a hurry to get away from this place," said Saya loudly, trying to catch other people's attention.

"You did? What did they look like?" asked the man with curiosity.

"One green haired male and one pink haired female," she replied.

"Hey, those are the creatures that attacked us earlier!" said a man from the next table who had been listening.

Soon everyone in the bar was talking about the Kelluas.

"And you definitely saw them?" another traveller asked Saya.

"Yes, I'm sure of it," replied Saya.

"We need to tell those girls with the swords!" shouted one man. "Maybe those crazy kids can go off and finish what they started. Better their problem than ours."

"Are they staying in the inn?" asked a woman from the back of the room.

"I think so," said another voice.

Several people ran out of the bar to go to the inn.

Mission accomplished, thought Saya triumphantly as she walked out of Tura to find a secluded place where she could teleport back to the hideout.

She found a quiet spot, and she was about to teleport when she heard someone come up behind her.

"You are Saya, am I right?"

She turned around to see one of the travellers she'd spoken to in the bar. His face was concealed by a woolly scarf and hat. He took them off, revealing his face.

Saya gasped when she realised who it was.

His hair was a different colour and the distinguishing facial mark was gone, but there was no mistaking his identity. It was Kyros.

"What... what are you doing here? And what happened to your hair?" she stammered.

Kyros smiled, and Saya realised she'd never seen him smile before. While he was with the Kelluas, he had always been depressed about his inferiority to everyone else. "Pretty simple, actually. I became human," said Kyros, shrugging. "Humans don't have naturally blue hair, so I guess it turned into a normal blonde shade."

He spoke as if it was the most natural thing in the world, but to Saya the idea of becoming human repulsed her.

"What do you want?" Saya sneered. "I was about to return to the hideout."

"You're still with the Superior?" Kyros asked, surprised. "I thought you didn't like following orders."

"I don't like following orders, but it's not like I have a choice," she replied. "I don't want to become human like you. I wouldn't stoop so low."

"That's understandable," replied Kyros.

Kyros' calm attitude was really annoying Saya. To her it seemed like he was rubbing his freedom in her face.

"How are Michius and Oden?" Kyros asked.

Saya wondered if she should lie. She decided to tell the truth.

"They're both dead," she said, without emotion. "Michius was killed by a human, and Oden was killed by Corvus- I mean, the Superior."

"They're dead and you still want to work for the Superior after all he's done?" asked Kyros. "Isn't it obvious all he cares about is his own agenda? Even if you manage to survive, do you really think staying with him will make you happy?"

"Of course not," Saya muttered. She knew Kyros was right, but she was unsure of what to do next.

She was a Kellua. Physical descriptions of her had spread all over the continent; she had no chance of blending in and living a normal life. She would have to go back to the meaningless life she had lived before Corvus found her. Constantly in hiding and on the run from humans.

The obvious option was to become human. However, the prospect of being human scared Saya. She didn't want to join the sworn enemies of her ancestors.

"Listen, Saya," said Kyros, seriously. "Ever since becoming human I've been desperately searching for a purpose in life. The burden of what I did while I was still following the Superior became too great. I couldn't live with myself knowing the blood of innocent people was on my hands."

"But they deserved it, Kyros!" Saya cried. "The humans slaughtered our ancestors without mercy. All you did was destroy some tiny farming village!"

"The humans who destroyed our ancestors are gone now, Saya. They were obsessed with magic and destroying anyone more powerful than them. This new generation is different. Sure, many of them are still prejudiced. Both of us suffered in our childhoods for fear of being discovered.

But look at those girls. They forgave me as soon as I stopped working for the Superior, despite the fact I killed on of their sisters! These humans are driven by love, not hate."

"Please spare me the bleeding heart routine," Saya groaned. "They only accepted you because you stopped being a Kellua."

"You don't understand, Saya," Kyros pleaded. "You need to learn forgiveness. When I was drowning in my guilt I met some humans who called themselves 'Christians'. They told me about the One True God, and how he sent his Son, Jesus Christ, to die on Earth to forgive the sins of all creation. That includes Kelluas too, even though we were not born on Earth. I was sceptical at first but once I came to believe this and learned how to forgive, I placed my trust In Jesus and my burden was immediately lifted."

"Good for you, you've become so human you're even beginning to believe in their myths. Tell me Kyros, how does any of this spiritual mumbo jumbo affect me?" asked Saya dubiously.

"Saya, as soon as I was saved I tried to find you. It's a shame Oden and Michius aren't here too, but at least I have a chance to share the good news of Jesus with you," he explained. "Look, I know we've never seen eye-to-eye on anything, but you've got to trust me on this. This isn't a trick. Aren't you tired of being the Superior's slave? If you want know what it means to be free, repent of your sins and join me."

The stubborn side of Saya wanted to reject Kyros' plea. Her heart was hardened against humans after the abuse she had suffered in her childhood and she refused to believe this new generation was any different. However, a small part of her longed to feel the sort of peace Kyros described.

"I'll strike a deal with you," she decided. "I'll leave the Superior and join you. However, I'm not buying into any of your ridiculous God stuff."

This is interesting. I didn't expect her to be convinced straight away, thought Kyros. *It took me a while, I imagine it will take her much longer. But at least she's willing to leave the Superior. That's a huge step in the right direction.*

"That's fine," he replied. "You know I'm no good at fighting, especially now I have no Kellua abilities anymore. I'd much rather have you as an ally rather than an enemy. However, I must beg you to abandon your powers and to become human."

Saya folded her arms defiantly. This was where she would draw the line.

"Why should I? You were saying earlier it didn't matter if I was Kellua or human. I don't believe it but you said this Jesus died for all of creation."

"It doesn't make a difference in terms of your salvation, but you'll always be wanted by the Superior as long as you're a Kellua as long as you are capable of helping him regenerate our kind. You'll be in constant danger," he explained, solemnly. "Honestly Saya, being human isn't as bad as you would think."

Being exploited by Corvus is perhaps the only fate worse than being human, she thought.

"Fine. I'll do it," she agreed, reluctantly.

As Kyros had done, Saya raised her hands and channelled all of her energy into them. She silenced her doubts and focused on the process at hand. A light shone around her hands and became steadily brighter until she could no longer look at it. She released it and watched regretfully as her powers dissipated into the air.

"What... What have I done?" she muttered before collapsing into the snow, fully human.

Kyros threw her over his shoulder and staggered towards the Tura inn. Despite the burden, he felt a sense of relief. The fight against The Superior had gained another ally.

***

After the giant snowball fight Hikari, Kerry, Rhianna and Noi were sitting in front of the fire in the inn, attempting to dry their clothes. Having been informed by the bar patrons of where to find the Kellua, they knew they would have to leave for the Northern Mountains as soon as possible, but they weren't foolish enough to walk up snow covered mountains in soaking wet clothes. The people in Tura had been very kind to them, and they had given the girls and Noi plenty of non-perishable food for their journey.

Hikari hoped the Kellua's base was hidden somewhere in the mountains. That way they could finally challenge the leader of the Kellua to a final battle, and then her quest for vengeance would be complete.

The door to the inn opened and a young man walked in. His face was mostly obscured by the scarf and hat he was wearing, and he was carrying an unconscious girl over his shoulder.

The innkeeper immediately got to her feet and rushed over to help. Collapsed travellers were a common occurrence, and she knew exactly how to deal with situations such as this one. She led the man, Kyros, into one of the spare rooms, where he laid Saya down on the bed.

Kyros wasn't particularly concerned for her, because he knew when he lost his own powers he was only unconscious for a few hours. He hadn't even noticed Hikari, Kerry, Rhianna and Noi were in the inn.

"Do you think that girl was alright?" said Kerry, oblivious to the fact the unconscious girl was actually Saya.

"She probably got frostbite or something," said Noi. "I'm sure she'll be fine."

"We should take that as a warning to be extra careful on the mountains, then," said Hikari. "We don't want to end up like her."

The others agreed, and they waited for their clothes to finish drying.

Eventually, at around midday, they were ready to head out. Rhianna went to pay the innkeeper, but she shook her head and said their stay was on the house.

"That was nice," said Kerry, as they walked out of the inn into the cold outside air. "Being a group of insane sword wielding girls pays off sometimes."

Noi deliberately coughed.

"Sorry," said Kerry, "Make that a group of sword wielding girls and their chef."

Noi sighed.

"Is that all I am to you?" he said jokingly.

"Take it as a compliment!" Kerry said with a smile.

They walked out of Tura and onto the beaten path leading into the Northern Mountains. The air was crisp and cold, and they could see their breath condense into the air around them. The path led them through a snowfield and they could see nothing around them except for white snow blanketing the barren landscape and stretching as far as the eye could see. In the distance, they could see the ominous outline of the Northern Mountains.

Climbing the mountains is going to be fun, thought Hikari as she walked along the path. *I hope the rumours were correct. Otherwise, we are wasting our time.*

They walked along the path for a long while and exchanged small talk along the way. Gradually, the path started to get steeper and before they knew it they were deep within the mountains, searching relentlessly for any sign of Kelluas or a Kellua hideout. Steep cliffs towered over them on either side of the path.

Meanwhile, atop one of those very cliffs, Corvus looked down upon the girls and Noi, grinning to himself.

I'm not sure why Saya never returned, but it appears she completed her mission by successfully leading these gullible kids into my trap. Eliminating them will be easier than I thought. Once they are dead, I will see to tracking down Saya. Together, we shall repopulate this world with a new generation of Kellua and the humans will be our slaves.

So much to do, but completing the experiment and restoring my natural powers will be a cakewalk once these meddlesome kids are out of the way.

The snow was beginning to fall heavier. Corvus spotted the perfect place to execute his plan. There was an outcrop of rock hanging precariously over the path below, and it was all that was stopping a huge pile of fresh snow covered rock from falling.

Only one shot, and it should all come tumbling down.

He waited until Hikari, Kerry, Rhianna and Noi were in the right spot.

"I'm so tired..." moaned Kerry, as she walked at a slower pace than the others.

"Keeping moving!" shouted Hikari from the front. "If you slow down, you'll only get cold!"

Hikari walked right under where Corvus was targeting.
Now!

He shot black orbs of energy at the outcrop.

"Race you!" Hikari yelled at Kerry. She ran out of the avalanche's danger zone, and so did Rhianna and Noi.

"Race where…?" asked Kerry, as she slowly trudged along. "We don't even know where we're going."

Kerry heard the sound of impact above her.

Hikari turned around to see what the noise was about and she gasped, terrified, as she saw the outcrop above Kerry begin to fall away.

"Run Kerry!" yelled Rhianna, but Kerry stayed put, petrified as a massive wave of snow fell from the cliffs above. She started to run, but it was too late. She was quickly buried by the avalanche.

Corvus swore as he watched from the top of the cliff, hiding behind a rock. He wanted to kill all of them, not just one.

"Kerry!!!" Rhianna shrieked, running towards the snow pile.

Rhianna started digging into the snow, desperately trying to get Kerry out. She managed to uncover her hand, which was abnormally pale.

"Help me!!!" she yelled at Hikari and Noi, who were standing still in shock.

They ran to Rhianna's side and together they joined in the effort to rescue Kerry.

Corvus watched from above, annoyed with himself for not killing them all. He considered ambushing them as they tried to rescue Kerry, but he didn't feel like having a three against one fight. Without the full strength of his Kellua powers, he knew he would have to prepare and train more before he was confident enough to confront them directly.

The sun pulled across the sky as the girls and Noi tried to rescue Kerry. Rhianna brushed away the last of the snow covering her. She was still and unmoving, and Rhianna started to sob uncontrollably. Noi pushed Rhianna out of the way, and checked Kerry's wrist for a pulse.

"She's still alive," he announced. "We need to get her somewhere warm, quickly."

Noi turned to Rhianna, who was still crying.

"Is there a village near here, or is going back to Tura our only hope?"

Hikari was surprised at how calm and collected Noi was being compared to herself and Rhianna.

Rhianna dug her map out of her bag with trembling hands. She looked at it, and shook her head.

"Tura is our only option," she said.

"Then Tura it is," said Noi, and he lifted Kerry over his shoulder.

He ran as fast as he could in the direction of Tura, and Hikari and Rhianna followed behind.

Walking downhill it only took a few hours to reach Tura, but it felt like forever.

Hikari was enraged at herself for being so stupid.

I went up here based on nothing but a rumour. I knew it was dangerous, yet I still insisted we go. Kerry's condition is my fault.

They reached Tura as the sun went down. Noi was very tired, but he didn't show it. Instead he was focused, driven. They rushed straight to the inn.

Since they had left town, Saya had recovered, and she was sitting by the fireplace with Kyros. As they watched Noi carry Kerry into the inn, followed by Rhianna and Hikari, Saya and Kyros knew Corvus was involved somehow.

Saya remembered she was the one who convinced them to go up the mountains. When she saw Kerry, and saw how worried her friends were, she experienced a feeling she had never felt before.

Guilt.

Up until now they had been her enemies, but now she realised they should no longer be her adversaries. They were both the same race now, and they shared a common goal. They all wanted to defeat Corvus.

Noi carried Kerry into one of the rooms in the inn the innkeeper reserved for collapsed travellers. It was the same room Saya had been in only a few hours before.

Hikari hastily explained to the innkeeper what had happened, while Noi laid Kerry down on the bed.

The innkeeper looked worried.

She was used to dealing with exhaustion, frostbite, dehydration and other common ailments that travellers developed while climbing the mountains, but she wasn't used to dealing with avalanche victims. Avalanches were common on the mountains, but usually the people buried by them were instantly killed.

"She has severe hypothermia," said the innkeeper, after taking Kerry's pulse and checking her temperature. "She's lucky she wasn't further in, or the weight of the snow would have killed her instantly."

The innkeeper took off Kerry's wet clothes and replaced them with dry clothes Rhianna retrieved from her bag. The innkeeper knew the most important thing was to help Kerry regain body heat, so she ordered Hikari to light the fireplace in the corner of the room. She then ordered Rhianna and Noi to fill buckets with water and boil them over the fire. When this was done, she placed them against Kerry's clothes.

The method seemed weird to Rhianna and Hikari, but they trusted the innkeeper knew what she was doing. However, to Noi, seeing this type of treatment was nothing new. When he lived in the Alburn orphanage, there were a lot of cases of hypothermia among the younger boys during winter, although none of them had been as ill as Kerry. He knew the purpose of the buckets was to allow the person to slowly regain body heat. They weren't put directly on the skin, as that would cause burns and the patient would regain heat too quickly, which could shock the heart.

Noi was surprised he still remembered something he had been taught. For the first time in his life, he felt perhaps his education wasn't completely useless.

Despite the appropriate treatment, there was no sign of Kerry regaining consciousness.

Hikari had withdrawn herself into the corner of the room. She was reminded of the time when her mother was dying. She was terrified of losing another important person in her life.

She wanted to help in any way, but there was nothing she could do. She had no knowledge of how to treat hypothermia, and all the methods the innkeeper and Noi tried to revive her failed.

There's nothing I can do. It's like when Liza died. I couldn't do anything except watch her die. I can't save Kerry, and I couldn't save Liza, Honif, or my parents. I'm useless.

Unless....

Hikari remembered a conversation she had had with Kerry a few days ago. A conversation about prayer. She still had her doubts, but it seemed like there was no other option. She closed her eyes, and tried to remember how her family used to pray. As she began, Hikari felt a strange sensation. It was not the same as the repetitive and empty prayers she used to utter. It was led by the Holy Spirit.

Dear Heavenly Father,

I know I've been bad. I know I've sinned.

Please save Kerry. We need her. I need her. She can't die!

Forgive me for not believing in you, Lord. My suffering is more than I can bear alone. I'm weak and broken, I don't deserve your love. I deserve to be in Kerry's place.

I believe Christ died for me and rose from the dead. I'm tired of denying the truth. I am ready to trust in Him as my saviour.

If it is your will, please bring Kerry back to us.

In Jesus' name,

Amen

Hikari opened her tear-stained eyes. Her words had surprised even herself, but she knew they were genuine.

Rhianna was sitting on a stool beside Kerry's bed, sobbing quietly. Noi was standing back and watching, with a depressed look on his face. Kerry was always the happy one, the one who could cheer everyone up when they were sad. Without her, the world seemed a darker place.

Suddenly, Rhianna gasped.

Hikari looked at what had made her gasp, and she too was shocked.

Kerry had opened her eyes.

"Kerry!" yelled Rhianna, sounding extremely happy.

Hikari ran over to her bedside with joy.

Noi stayed back and watched the girls, and he smiled to himself. He was a sucker for happy endings.

"Wh... What happened?" asked Kerry in a daze. She couldn't understand why she was in a bed with hot buckets of water surrounding her. The last thing she remembered was walking in the Northern Mountains.

"You got buried underneath an avalanche!" cried Rhianna, who had quickly transitioned from tears of sorrow to weeping for joy.

"I what? Snappytaps, is that true?" asked Kerry, still extremely confused.

Hikari laughed at Kerry's use of her stupid nickname for her.

"Yes, you did," she said, "and you scared us all half to death."

"You know, if you'd walked faster you would've missed it," said Noi, from the corner of the room.

"Glad you're so concerned, Noi," said Kerry, jokingly.

"For your information, it was Noi who carried you all the way back to Tura," said Rhianna, matter-of-factly. "You owe him a lot of thanks."

"Wait, Tura??" said Kerry, surprised. "Why are we back in Tura? What about finding the Kellua hideout?"

"You are a bit more important than finding the Kelluas, Kerry," said Noi.

Rhianna continued to talk to Kerry, overjoyed her sister was well again. Noi went to tell the innkeeper Kerry had regained consciousness.

Hikari was amazed.

Christ really did hear my plea... He really is the Saviour of all worlds.

Liza's smiling face came to Hikari's mind, and her heart hardened.

Then why did Liza die? Why must there always be suffering?

Hikari had a lot of questions for Kerry when she was up to answering them.

Chapter 11

Meanwhile, Saya and Kyros watched Noi rush into the front room and tell the innkeeper Kerry had woken up.

Saya couldn't help feeling relieved. She wasn't sure if she could live with the burden of having killed someone.

When I was a Kellua, killing someone didn't seem like a big deal, although I never did kill a human. How come I'm suddenly so... humane? This must be part of becoming fully human. I'm beginning to understand why Kyros was so burdened. I always dismissed him as a weakling I could pick on whenever I wanted. He seems so much stronger and more serious now.

"She woke up, huh?" said Kyros, warming his hands over the fire.

"Yes," said Saya, not hiding how relieved she was, "I'm glad."

Kyros nodded, and he smiled.

"It's strange, but I think those kids are our allies now," he said, "although I'm not sure if they'd see us that way."

"We really should talk to them, and explain about Corvus and everything," said Saya, "and I really should apologise about misleading them up the mountain."

Kyros laughed.

"Wow, Saya apologising," he remarked. "That's something I never thought I'd hear."

Saya picked up the fire tongs that lay on the fireplace and pretended to threaten Kyros with them.

"Any more remarks like that, and I'll attack you with these. Remember, you're human now and humans bleed," she grinned.

"Now that's the Saya I know," Kyros laughed. "And you're right. We really should talk to those kids."

Saya nodded and set the fire tongs down. She was worried what they would think of her.

Of course, I'm assuming the avalanche was Corvus' fault. It could have been an accident.

No, it was far too convenient to be coincidence. He asks me to lead them to the mountains, and then they're struck by an avalanche? He must have done it.

Kyros walked into the corridor and knocked on the door of the room Saya had been in hours before, the room where Kerry now was. The innkeeper opened the door.

"Who is it? I'm busy, if you'd like a room..." said the innkeeper.

"We already have a room," interrupted Kyros. "We would like to visit the girl who was involved in the accident."

"Hey is that... Kyros?" asked Rhianna, surprised.

"Let him in," said Kerry.

With Liza fresh on her mind, Hikari couldn't help but scowl. She still deeply resented Kyros, even if Rhianna and Kerry had forgiven him. As for Noi, he hadn't even met Kyros before.

Noi entered the room, with Saya trailing awkwardly behind him.

Kerry was about to ask who the girl was, but she quickly realised it was Saya.

"Did you remove your powers too, Saya?" she asked in disbelief.

Saya nodded.

"We both decided following Corvus was the wrong thing to do," said Saya. "So we are now trying to bring him down."

"Corvus? Is he the Kellua leader?" asked Rhianna.

Kyros nodded. "Yes, but he's a leader no more. Corvus no longer has any Kelluas to command."

Hikari continued to sulk in the corner. Thinking about Liza and the unfairness of her sister's death made her want to wring Kyros' neck. Regardless of whether it was his fault or not, she should have made him pay for what he did to Liza.

"We need to talk to you about very important things regarding Corvus and his experiment," said Kyros, urgently. "But first, Saya wants to tell you something."

Saya blushed, and wondered what she should say.

"I'm sorry!" she blurted out. "I'm sorry for leading you into the mountains!"

"Wait..." said Hikari, with obvious hostility in her voice. "You were behind this?"

Her anger rose.

"I'm sorry!" repeated Saya, for the third time. "Corvus wanted me to lead you into the mountains, so I started the rumour about myself and Oden being in the mountains. I met Kyros on my way back to the hideout, and he convinced me to give up my powers and leave Corvus. When I saw you carrying that girl into the inn and I overheard what happened to her, only then did I regret what I had done. I knew Corvus was behind the avalanche, he must have been."

"'That girl' has a name," snapped Hikari. "She's called Kerry."

"I'm honestly very sorry, Kerry," said Saya.

Kerry smiled, instantly forgiving Saya.

"It's alright. I'm not dead or anything, so all is good!"

Hikari marvelled at Kerry's attitude.

All they had to do was apologise, and she forgave them without a second thought. Before I used to think I'd never be able to forgive Kyros as long as I lived. Maybe now I've accepted Jesus things will be different… It's definitely going to be hard.

Saya smiled, pleased Kerry had forgiven her.

"Now everything is settled, let's move onto the more serious business of why we must speak to you," said Kyros.

Hikari, Kerry, Rhianna and Noi listened intently as Kyros and Saya told them all about Corvus and his objectives. They told them about his need for a child's soul in order to complete the experiment. They also explained how Corvus had convinced the other Kelluas into joining his cause by getting them to believe it was the only way they would ever be free to live their lives without fear of discover and persecution.

Hikari's anger at Saya and Kyros softened slightly when she recognised they really were trying to repent by helping to take down Corvus. She still wasn't sure if she wanted to travel with them though. She decided she would go along with whatever Kerry, Rhianna and Noi decided.

Noi was the first to speak his opinion on what Saya and Kyros said.

"That really does explain a lot." he said. "I didn't know much about the Kelluas before, but I think the picture is clearer now. I am happy you two have decided to leave Corvus. You could be valuable allies when it comes to taking him down."

Hikari cringed at this. She hated to hear her former enemies described as allies so quickly.

"Are you going to join us?" asked Rhianna.

"Would you accept us into your fold?" asked Kyros, clearly surprised by the invitation.

Rhianna looked at Hikari.

"What do you say, Hikari?"

Hikari thought for a moment.

"They can join us," she said, after much thought.

Noi's right. They will be powerful allies. I should forget my grudges against them and be happy two more have joined the fight against Corvus. It's six against one now. This should be an easy victory.

"Do you know where the Kellua hideout is?" asked Kerry.

"Of course," replied Kyros. "It's just- oh, dear..."

"What is it?" asked Hikari.

"I forgot we can't teleport anymore. I know where the hideout is, but it will literally take days and days of walking to reach it."

Saya moaned.

"Why didn't we think of that before we gave up our powers?" she said. "And even if we did walk all the way to the hideout, Corvus isn't an idiot. He knows you're pursuing him and he might even guess you have our help. I expect he will clear out of there pretty soon. Walking so far to find an empty hideout would be pointless."

"So you're saying heading towards the hideout wouldn't be a sensible course of action?" asked Rhianna.

"I believe that's correct, yes," said Kyros, feeling a bit dejected.

By this time it was late at night and the innkeeper suggested Kerry should get some rest. Hikari was desperate to share the news of her salvation with Kerry once she had recovered. The others went off to their rooms and tried to get a good night's sleep.

***

As she was getting to sleep, Saya found herself reflecting on how she had joined Corvus in the first place.

Ever since she could remember, it had only been Saya and her mother. They had spent their lives living in the valleys at the very west of the Maysea Continent, foraging for food in human towns. Saya's mother didn't have any resentment towards humans, but every time she entered a town she was scorned and chased away by angry humans, who knew Saya's mother was a Kellua because of her un-humanlike pink hair.

Saya remembered making friends with a human girl once, when she was only about four years old. Saya and her mother had been walking through a valley that was next to a human town and they stopped to rest. When they stopped, Saya wandered off and found the girl playing on her own in the valley. She had hand-painted wooden dolls, and Saya had never seen anything like it.

She wanted to play with the girl, but her mother found her and sternly told her she must never mix with humans, no matter how nice they seemed. Saya adhered to this rule for years, until one day when she was ten.

She and her mother were back in the same area, near the same town, and they had found a sheltered spot in a forest to rest for the night. Saya's mother quickly fell asleep, but Saya couldn't sleep at all. She wandered out of the forest, and found herself in the same valley she had been in six years ago.

The human girl was also there, but instead of wooden dolls she had real sheep with her, and she held a wooden staff in her hand. She was a shepherd, but Saya didn't know what that was. The shepherd girl noticed Saya, and she had asked her where she came from. Saya had honestly replied that she didn't really know where she came from.

The human girl remembered being warned by her father to never talk to someone if they lived in the wilderness and had strangely coloured hair, just like Saya remembered her mother telling her not to go near humans. However, the two girls started talking and found that the other was nowhere near as bad as their parents had made out. Neither of the girls knew someone their own age, and they happily talked in the moonlight.

This was all brought to an abrupt end when the human girl's father came into the valley to take over the shepherding duties from his daughter. When he saw his daughter was talking to a Kellua, he was terrified. At around the same time Saya's mother entered the valley, looking for her daughter.

Saya didn't realise how serious the situation was, and she happily started talking to her mother.

"This is Grace," she said, pointing at the human girl. "She's a human, but she's really nice!"

Saya's mother ignored her daughter, too shocked at what she was seeing to reply.

"Grace! Get away from those two at once!" yelled Grace's father. "They're going to kill you!"

Saya's mother stamped her foot in indignation.

"Why would we do that?" she asked. "I know our race fought with yours in the past, but why can't we move on? Why are our children more sensible than we are?"

The man ignored her and yelled at his daughter.

"Go back home!"

"I don't want to! Saya is my friend!" protested Grace.

"Go home. Now!" her father repeated, snatching the wooden staff from her hand.

Grace started to cry and she ran back towards the human town.

"That was unnecessary," said Saya's mother in disgust.

"Get out of here. Don't come near this town again," snarled the man.

Saya's mother was ready to accept defeat and take Saya back into the woods, but Saya took off towards the human town.

"I'm tired of hiding. I don't want to live outside anymore!" she cried as she ran towards the town.

Saya's mother chased after her, trying to protect Saya from the hostile humans who lived in the town.

People screamed when they saw the two Kelluas in their town. None of the townspeople were old enough to remember the actual war between Kelluas and humans, but plenty of stories had been passed down across generations, getting more twisted and exaggerated with each telling.

Saya's memory of what happened next was unclear. She remembered her mother calling her name and telling her to get out of the town, but she didn't listen. It was then a man came out with a sword, and before Saya could do anything, her mother was dead. The crowd cheered on the man with the sword and frightened little Saya ran as fast as she could away from that town. Her hatred of humans started there.

For years she lived on her own, foraging and hunting to survive. One day when she was walking through a forest in the west of the continent, she met Corvus. Until that moment she thought she was the only Kellua left, and she was thrilled to see another one was still alive. She was even more thrilled when he said he had already recruited one more Kellua – Michius. Corvus explained his plan, and how he wanted to reclaim what the humans had taken from them.

Saya, still furious at all humans whom she blamed for the death of her mother, agreed to go with him.

As Saya lay awake in the Tura inn, she couldn't help but wonder if any of the other Kelluas serving under Corvus had similar back stories.

At last, she finally drifted off to sleep.

***

When morning came, they all met in front of the fireplace in the front room. Noi had baked bread for everyone's breakfast to save the innkeeper from doing it, as a way of thanking her for taking care of Kerry.

"How on Maysea did all six of you end up joining me?" said Hikari, amazed by the amount of people who had rallied to her cause in such a short time.

"The more the merrier, right?" said Kerry, while eating her fourth slice of bread.

Kyros and Saya were also eating numerous slices of Noi's bread. Kelluas didn't have huge appetites, and could go far longer than humans without food. However, now they were human, Kyros and Saya were utterly famished.

"Corvus is going to have to show himself now," Saya said. "He can't hide behind his pawns any more. Are there any nearby towns? If he's still trying to seize a child, we need to catch him before he is successful."

"There's one called Musura," said Rhianna, squinting at the map. "It's not too far from here. Everything after that is wilderness."

"That should be our next port of call then," said Saya.

"Agreed," replied Rhianna. "If everyone is ready, we should head out."

They all got up and got ready to go, and Kerry eventually dragged herself off the armchair she was sitting on as well. Kerry thanked the innkeeper for taking care of her, and they stepped out into the cold.

"I'm getting a strange feeling of déjà vu," joked Kerry. "It seems every time we try to leave this village we end up coming back."

"I'm not saying I don't like Tura or anything, but let's hope this is the last time we visit it," said Rhianna.

"Or at least make sure one of us isn't half dead next time we visit," laughed Hikari.

"Oh yes, you all make fun at my expense," said Kerry, laughing. "You were obviously so worried about me."

"Seriously though, you were pretty bad," said Noi. "Don't push yourself. It wouldn't be the same without you around."

"Heh, thanks..." replied Kerry, blushing slightly. "I'm one of a kind."

They walked southwest away from Tura along a narrow path connecting it to Musura, the closest town. As they walked on the temperature began to rise and eventually they were able to take off some of the numerous layers of winter clothing they were wearing. A pattern in walking speeds emerged, with Kyros and Saya at the front, Rhianna and Noi in the middle, and Hikari and Kerry lagging behind.

As they proceeded through plains and forests, they found the terrain was fairly easy to walk on. Kerry was especially grateful they didn't have to walk uphill. Time passed uneventfully until they were in the middle of a forest and a strange creature jumped out in front of them.

It resembled an alligator, but it managed to walk on its hind legs while waving its sharply clawed front legs at them. It was undoubtedly a monster, and it bared its teeth at the travellers.

"Time to fight!" yelled Hikari, dodging out of the way of the monster as it leapt off the ground and tried to bite her arm.

Everyone drew their weapons and they surrounded the creature. Fighting was becoming much easier now, due to a combination of their increased numbers and all the training they had done. The creature panicked for a moment before launching itself in Noi's direction. He slashed the creature with his sword, and it fell to the ground, stunned. Hikari then delivered the final attack, and the monster disintegrated into the ground.

"Eww…" said Kerry.

"You know nearly 20% of soil is made up of monster remains, right?" asked Rhianna. "And you eat food that grows in the soil."

"That's gross!" exclaimed Kerry. "You mean I've been eating disintegrated monsters?"

"Pretty much, yes," replied Rhianna.

"Ewwwwwwwwwwwwwwwwww!" cried Kerry, and she started desperately drinking out of her water canteen and spitting on the ground, as if there were actually disintegrated monsters in her mouth.

The others sat down and had a drink as well. It was nearly midday, but according to Rhianna's map they were still nowhere near their destination.

"Let's try to reach this point before we take a break," said Rhianna, pointing to a spot on the map that was on the outskirts of the forest they were in. It was right next to a stream, which would be useful for refilling water canteens and other things.

Everyone else agreed and they walked on through the forest, alert in case any other monsters tried to attack them.

The forest was thick with trees, and at one point a tree's roots had expanded out over the path, which caused Kerry to trip and fall on her face.

"Are you alright?" said Rhianna, concerned.

"Yeah, thanks," said Kerry, as she stood up and brushed the dirt off her clothes.

"That was a pretty spectacular fall," said Noi, laughing.

"You... You're in for it now, Noi!" yelled Kerry, and she started chasing Noi down the path.

"How come she only has that sort of energy when she's angry?" remarked Rhianna.

They walked on, with Kerry and Noi far ahead of everyone else.

"What do you think Kerry will do if she actually catches him?" Hikari asked Rhianna.

"Probably trip him up to get revenge," said Rhianna.

"I can't decide if Kerry hates Noi or likes him," laughed Hikari.

"Perhaps chasing him and making him fall on his face is Kerry's special way of showing affection," said Rhianna with a smile.

They eventually caught up with Kerry and Noi. Kerry was sitting down on the path, tired from all the running she did. Noi was brushing dirt off his clothes that had got there when Kerry tripped him up three times.

"Keep that sister of yours on a leash, she's mental!" said Noi to Rhianna.

"Yup, that's Kerry alright..." said Rhianna, shaking her head.

"How much further before we reach the stream?" asked Kerry. "I'm tired."

"You're always tired," Noi pointed out.

"Do you want me to trip you up three more times?" asked Kerry, hands on her hips.

"Uh... I'm good, thanks," said Noi, quickly.

Rhianna pulled out her map.

"I'd say we should reach the stream in about an hour," said Rhianna, and she rolled the map back up and placed it in her bag.

"An hour...." grumbled Kerry as she got to her feet. "Let's get moving then. The sooner we get there, the sooner we can rest."

As they walked out of the forest the trees that had once formed a thick canopy over their heads thinned out until they were out of the forest altogether.

"I can see the stream!" yelled Kerry, pointing to the faint line of blue in the distance. Seeing their destination was so close gave Kerry a boost of energy, and she started running towards the stream with the others following.

They reached the stream, and they all immediately filled their water containers and had a drink. Kerry and Hikari were out of the earshot of the others, so Hikari took this as an opportunity to speak to Kerry in private.

"Hey, Kerry..." Hikari said, awkwardly. "About that stuff you were talking to me about a few days ago.... Christianity and all that..."

"Yeah, what about it?" said Kerry enthusiastically, happy Hikari was taking an interest.

"After you were injured on the Northern Mountains, we didn't really think you'd ever regain consciousness," said Hikari. "I felt really alone then, like there was nothing good left in the world. It was during that moment I started to pray for you to be better. And I asked Jesus to be my saviour. Then you woke up."

Kerry squealed with happiness and threw her arms around Hikari.

"I'm so happy, Snappytaps!" she cried. "I've been waiting for this moment for a long time!"

"Have you had prayers answered before?" asked Hikari, returning the embrace.

"Oh yeah," said Kerry. "In fact, when I lived in Dunin I got so bored I used to pray for something interesting and exciting to happen. Then you came along!"

"I came to Dunin because Honif was destroyed. Nothing to do with your prayers," said Hikari, sceptically.

"But, you see, God works in mysterious ways. You could be answering other people's prayers every day, without even realising it," Kerry explained.

"So you're saying Honif getting destroyed was to answer your prayer, then?" said Hikari, getting angry like she always did when talking about Honif.

"No! Not at all!" said Kerry quickly. "I'm saying good things can come out of even the direst of events. Pain makes people stronger."

"How would you know?" shouted Hikari. "You've never experienced pain as bad as what I went through, and what I'm still going through!"

She had shouted loud enough for the others to hear, and they turned around to see what was going on.

"Yes, life is full of amazing things," said Hikari, still shouting even though the others were staring at her. "But why then is there is so much suffering? Explain that with your fancy theology, why don't you!"

Kerry was speechless at Hikari's outburst.

Hikari felt tears start to form in her eyes and she took off in a random direction, wanting to get as far away from everyone and everything as possible.

I've been happy for the past few weeks. But it was all superficial. I've never stopped hurting on the inside this entire time. Being friends with this lot helped me forget about what really happened, but the truth is I have no life to return to when this is all over.

I pledged to put my trust in Jesus, but I'm still so confused. I have so many unanswered questions. Why, Lord? Why did Liza have to die?

It started to rain. Hikari barely noticed the cold water soaking through her clothes. She tripped on an uneven part of the path and fell to her knees.

"Hikari!" yelled Rhianna as she ran towards her, rain dripping off her hair.

"Go away!" yelled Hikari, crying and still on her knees. "I don't want to see any of you!"

"It's only a few miles to Musura," said Noi, who wasn't good at dealing with awkward friendship disputes. "I'm not sure what's going on between you two, but it's going to get really wet and cold. Whatever needs to be sorted out can be done when we get to Musura."

Rhianna nodded at what Noi said.

"Let's get to Musura," she said, softly.

Rhianna's kindness annoyed Hikari even more, and she got off the ground and started marching back towards the path, ignoring everyone.

Rhianna shot Kerry a confused look.

"What happened?" Rhianna asked.

Kerry shook her head.

"It can be discussed later," said Kerry. "We need to run after Hikari."

They caught up with her and then continued their walk to Musura in awkward silence.

What on Maysea happened? thought Rhianna, baffled. *Hikari was so happy when Kerry woke up, why is she suddenly so annoyed at her?*

The town of Musura came into view, and Saya gasped when she saw it. The rows of terraced housing with distinctively flat roofs were all too familiar.

"What's wrong with you?" asked Kyros, when he saw Saya's expression.

"This place… something happened here in my past," she whispered.

Saya hadn't told Kyros about what happened to her when she was younger. She hadn't told anyone. She was worried she might run into the man with the sword who killed her mother.

Saya also wondered if Grace still lived in Musura, and if she did, would Grace still recognise her?

Of course she won't, thought Saya. *I don't have neon pink hair anymore.*

Saya hoped Hikari would quickly get over whatever was causing her to feel down like she was, because she didn't want to stay in this town a second longer than necessary. It was associated with too many dark memories.

The group walked into Musura, a normal small-sized town. It was late afternoon, and many people were walking along the paved streets. The houses were tall and the upper stories jutted out over the street. Tradesmen stood in the streets advertising their various businesses in loud, booming voices. It was a very busy town, despite its size.

They walked until they found an inn, and they bought a couple of rooms for the night. Rhianna, Kerry and Noi then sat down with Hikari to talk to her about what had caused her outburst. Saya quietly crept out of the inn when she was sure no-one was looking.

Kyros didn't want to be involved with whatever was troubling Hikari, so he wandered around the town, looking at various stalls in the market place.

Back at the inn, Kerry was talking to Rhianna about the conversation she had had with Hikari before she ran off. Hikari was sitting in the corner of the room in silence. She wasn't angry anymore, just depressed, as if everything she had done in the past few weeks had never happened. Her eyes were lifeless.

Rhianna sighed after Kerry explained everything.

Rhianna would have described herself as Christian, because that was how she had been brought up. However, she wasn't quite as devout and serious about it as Kerry was. She only really attended church because she was expected to.

Rhianna knew if she had lost everything like Hikari had, she too would probably have little faith left in God.

How are we going to cheer Hikari up? I understand Kerry is keen for her to become a Christian, but I'm not sure if now is really an appropriate time. Then again, when would be an appropriate time?

***

Saya walked out of Musura and into the neighbouring plain. It was the same plain where she met Grace, many years ago. She observed the vast plain, which seemingly spread all the way out into the horizon. In the distance, she could make out the silhouettes of sheep. She started to run towards them, to see if Grace was really there. Saya decided that if Grace really was there she wouldn't talk to her. She only wanted to see if she was still alive and well.

As she got closer to the sheep, she could see the figure of the shepherd guarding them. She saw it really was Grace, and she was happy.

Grace looked older, but other than that she looked the same. She clutched a wooden staff in her hand and she had the same lonely look in her eyes she had had all those years ago. Saya felt sorry for her, having to stand outside all day, with nothing but the sheep for company. Saya wondered if Grace's father was still alive. She really hated that man, just as she hated the man with the sword. But she did not hate Grace.

Saya was about to turn away and go back to Musura, when Grace noticed her standing there.

"Are you lost?" Grace asked.

What do I do now? thought Saya. *Should I pretend to be a lost traveller, or should I tell her who I really am and hope she remembers me?*

She opted for the latter.

"I'm not lost," Saya explained. "I came to speak to you, Grace."

Grace looked shocked and a little scared when she realised the strange woman standing in front of her knew her name.

"My name is Saya. You probably have no idea who I am."

Grace thought for a second, and then her face lit up.

"Saya!" she cried. "As in Saya, the girl with pink hair?"

"That's me," said Saya. "However, as you can see, my hair isn't pink anymore."

Grace threw her arms around Saya.

"I've missed you," she said. "You were the only friend I ever had, even if it was only for a day."

Saya returned the hug. She had often thought of Grace, but she never thought she would actually meet her again.

Leaving Corvus seems to be a better decision with each passing day, thought Saya. *According to him, Grace should be my enemy. However, she's not. When I worked for Corvus, driven by my grief over losing my mother, I wanted to eradicate all humans. Now I realise how stupid and wrong my thinking was. There are bad humans, of course, but there are far more decent ones than bad.*

"You're still a shepherd, I see," said Saya, smiling. Grace nodded.

"I still am. I like it, but it can be a bit lonely."

"I can imagine," said Saya. "I don't exactly envy you."

"What have you been doing, Saya?" Grace asked.

You know, the usual. Like trying to destroy the entire human race, and then ending up siding with them. Normal, everyday things.

"Oh, just hanging out in the woods," Saya lied.

Grace smiled and the two girls talked with joy as if they were ten years old again and not a day had passed.

***

Meanwhile back at the inn, things weren't so happy.

"Come on, Hikari," begged Kerry. "Speak to us, would you?"

"I know it must be hard for you to come to terms with Liza's death," said Rhianna, kindly. "But for the past few weeks you've been happy around us. Don't stop now. Please."

Hikari was determined to stay in her secluded state.

"What's up with her? Is she sick?" Kerry asked, at a loss over what to do.

"I think she was supressing the truth while she was happy," said Rhianna. "Now the true impact of what happened to Liza has hit her. We were a sort of distraction for her, and she was able to be happy, but now she's depressed."

Kerry sighed for the thousandth time. She didn't like it when people were unhappy.

"How do we stop her being depressed, then?" asked Kerry.

"It's not that simple," said Rhianna. "The grieving process varies between individuals. It can take years to feel 'normal' again."

"Years?" moaned Kerry. "She can't strop in a corner for years!"

"We can't even begin to try and understand the pain she's going through, but we should try to lessen her burden in any way we can," said Rhianna, thoughtfully.

"How do we do that?" said Kerry.

"We need to restore her faith in this world, because right now she thinks everything is pointless," said Rhianna.

"We have to help her, just like she helped us," Kerry declared. "That's what friends do. Any ideas, Noi?"

Kerry turned to Noi, who had been watching the girls from the corner of the room without saying a word.

"Uhhh..." he said, unsure of what to say. "I don't know... Sorry..."

"He's as clueless as the rest of us," said Kerry.

Rhianna stood up and walked out of the room.

"Hey, where are you going?" Kerry asked.

"I can't think while cooped up in here. I need fresh air," Rhianna replied.

"Can I come?" asked Kerry, excitedly.

"Yes, of course," said Rhianna. "What about you Noi?"

"I'll stay here." he said. "I'll keep an eye on Hikari, in case she tries anything stupid."

"Good idea," said Rhianna as the two sisters left the inn.

Eventually the two sisters came to a group of market stalls, all colourfully decorated. Banners were hung from windows of the surrounding houses, and the whole place glowed with a sort of party atmosphere. Children ran between the stalls, squealing with excitement.

"Is this some sort of festival?" Kerry asked, looking around in amazement.

If there weren't more pressing matters to attend to, I really could spend all day here. It's amazing, thought Rhianna.

At one of the stalls Rhianna saw Kyros browsing a range of home baked pastries, and she called out to him.

"Look, it's Kyros!" she shouted, waving.

"Oh, hello," said Kyros. "Where are the rest?"

"Hikari and Noi are back at the inn," said Kerry. "I have no idea where Saya disappeared to."

Kyros nodded.

"She said this town was somehow connected to her past. There's probably a place she wants to revisit," said Kyros.

"Oh, I never realised," Rhianna replied.

Just as they were talking about her, Saya started walking towards them. She had finished talking to Grace, and had happened to stumble upon the festival on her way back to the inn.

Kyros waved when he saw her.

"Kyros?" Saya asked in surprise, as she walked towards Kyros, Kerry and Rhianna. "What are you all doing here?"

"It's a festival!" cried Kerry. "Why would we not be here?"

"Where were you, Saya?" Kyros asked.

"Visiting a friend," said Saya, not wanting to say any more about it.

Kyros nodded without asking the question that naturally came to mind.

"Hey, you two," said Rhianna to Saya and Kyros. "Could you help us cheer Hikari up?"

"She's still sulking?" asked Saya in disbelief.

"How can we help?" said Kyros, with a good deal more compassion than Saya.

"She's very upset, and she's shutting everything and everyone out," said Rhianna, sadly.

"That sounds quite familiar... There was a time when I was once like that," said Saya, looking at the ground.

"I was in a very dark place once, driven by my grief. That's what led me to join Corvus." Saya continued. "It was only when I abandoned my powers and became human I think I truly got over my sadness. I realised even if I had lost something extremely important to me, I still have people who care about me. Thank you for helping me realise this, Kyros."

Saya blushed, embarrassed at delivering such an emotional speech.

Kyros, Kerry and Rhianna were surprised. Especially Kyros.

He had never noticed Saya was grateful to him, as he had been under the impression Saya had only joined him because she didn't want to be with Corvus anymore.

"No need to thank me," Kyros said. "That's what friends do. We look out for one another. You know, when I was at my lowest a few weeks ago after giving up my powers, there was a book someone gave me that kept me from giving up hope."

Kyros reached into his bag and pulled out a book. It had a leather cover and was slightly worn around the edges. Kerry recognised it instantly.

She snapped her fingers.

"Why didn't I think of that?" she exclaimed. "May I see it, Kyros?"

He nodded and passed the book to her.

"This is the Bible, a book of God's holy scriptures. And I think it may well be the answer to Hikari's problem," she said. "She has already called out to be saved, but she's still got so many questions that need answered. Anything she needs will be in here."

Saya couldn't help but be sceptical. It was hard for her to view Christianity as anything other than human folklore. However, as she witnessed the effects it was having on the people around her she began to get a little curious. Perhaps she'd have to borrow that book too, to see what all the fuss was about.

Kerry marched determinately to the inn and the others quickly followed behind her. Hikari was still sitting in the corner of her room, moping and not responding to anything.

"Hey, Hikari."

No response.

"Hikarrrrrrrrrrrrrrrrrrrrrrrrrrrrrri?" she repeated.

Still no response.

Kerry got out Kyros' Bible and started flicking through the onion-skin pages. She said a quick and silent prayer, asking that the Holy Spirit would give her the right words to say.

"Fine, don't talk to me. You can listen. I believe deep down, you desire to put your trust in Christ to heal your pain, but your past still haunts you," she said. "This book here contains all you need to know about how to move forwards. I'm sure your family used to have one at home. It's called the Holy Bible."

Hikari remained silent, but shifted her gaze towards Kerry.

Kerry found the page she was looking for.

"See, God knows everything you're going through, Hikari. In Romans we are told, *'For I reckon that the sufferings of this present time are not worthy to be compared with the glory which shall be revealed in us,'"* she quoted. "One day you will leave this world behind to be with Christ, Hikari. You have to learn to trust in Him."

"There's another verse that was particularly helpful to me," Kyros joined in. "It was from Psalm 34: *'Many are the afflictions of the righteous: but the Lord delivereth him out of them all.'"*

The message touched not only Hikari's heart but also that of Saya and Noi, who had lived their whole lives without once considering the possibility of giving their pain to Jesus Christ.

"Also, Hikari. Look at how much you have been blessed," Kerry continued. "You're surrounded by people who love you and you've been to some awesome places. I know the rest of us can't even imagine what you're going through, but some people would eat their socks to be having the kind of adventure you are having now!"

Hikari thought about this and then, to everyone's surprise, she began to laugh. Her laughter quickly turned to tears when she realised how much everyone had supported her along her journey.

Kerry hugged Hikari, who sobbed in her arms.

"Th... Thank you, everyone," she stammered through her tears.

"You can keep that Bible," Kyros said. "I'll get another one. Right now you need it more than any of us."

Hikari received the Bible gratefully, still crying.

Noi watched from the background, smiling and feeling a bit misty eyed himself.

"Hikari, if you feel like letting your pals cheer you up, there's a festival on at the moment we could all go to," he said.

Hikari smiled and nodded. "I suppose it's time to stop feeling sorry for myself."

"Yay!" squealed Kerry, and she pulled Hikari to her feet. "Let's go!"

They ran (or got dragged, in Hikari's case) towards the festival. Once there, Hikari gazed in amazement at all the stalls and the lavish decorations. The food stalls were offering all sorts of delicious cuisine, including the sorts of food she used to eat at home.

A stall selling a whole range of colourful confectionary stall caught Kerry's eye. She bought bagfuls of the stuff and walked around the festival happily eating the sweets.

At one point, Kerry noticed although Hikari was happy, her friend appeared deep in thought.

"Kerry..." asked Hikari, hesitantly. "What happens to people after they die?"

Kerry smiled.

"If they've placed their trust in Christ, they are destined for heaven, where they will live with him forever!" she said. "Jesus said *'The only way to the Father* is through me.', and he also promised that, *"In my Father's house are many mansions: if it were not so, I would have told you. I go to prepare a place for you."* You will meet your family again, Hikari. I truly believe that."

Hikari smiled.

That's not so bad, thought Hikari. *I have to offer up my suffering to Christ, and try to take joy in knowing I'll see Liza again.*

"Anyway, don't stress about it," said Kerry. "You're saved now and no one can take your salvation away from you. Besides, there's so much awesome stuff to do here! Come on!"

Kerry dragged Hikari around many of the stalls and they bought loads of stuff, including pastries, cake, hand-knitted socks, clay pots and other things they would never need in their lives.

When they met up with the others at the end of the day, Rhianna started yelling at Kerry.

"Wh... What on Maysea did you buy?" she exclaimed, when she saw the amount of stuff Kerry was carrying in her arms.

"Lighten up, I was having fun!"

"Yeah, having fun blowing all your money," said Rhianna. "Also, how are we going to transport all this? It's not going in my bag!"

Hikari laughed at the two of them arguing.

"I know what you could do," said Hikari. "There was a man selling bags at one of the stalls, and if we run there now we should be able to buy one before he closes his stall. Then Kerry can carry all the stuff she buys!"

Kerry moaned.

"I don't want to carry my own stuff...."

"Well, tough," said Rhianna. "I'm certainly not carrying it, and I'm sure no-one else wants to either. What exactly is all that stuff?"

Hikari dragged Kerry back towards the bag stall, and she bought a bag big enough to contain all the items she purchased.

"You're so mean…" Kerry moaned, as she hoisted the backpack full of random items on her back.

Hikari laughed and they ran back to join the others.

"Ready to go back to the inn?" asked Rhianna.

"Ready when you are," replied Hikari.

As they started walking, a figure materialised before them. To Saya and Kyros it was an all too familiar figure. The jovial atmosphere they had been enjoying vanished and was replaced by a deep feeling of dread.

Corvus hovered before them, with his black cloak covering most of his body and his hat tipped over his brow. His evil smile was menacing.

"Corvus!" Saya shouted in recognition as she stepped backwards in disgust.

"Nice to see you again, traitors," he spat at Kyros and Saya. "You abandoned me; you even abandoned your race. You are both a disgrace, and I look forward to ending both of your existences."

"I'd rather die young than live as a Kellua under your command!" yelled Saya. "A life where all we do is cause people pain is not a life worth living!"

"You have all thwarted my plans enough," Corvus replied dismissively. "I shall meet you in a small village called Sudata. There, we will have our final showdown. Believe me when I say this, you will lose."

"Of course we accept, you monster!" yelled Rhianna.

"We gladly accept!" yelled Hikari. "We will destroy you, like you destroyed the lives of so many people! You've hurt humans; you've even hurt your own kind. You're despicable!"

"Spare me the theatrics, my dear. I shall eagerly await your arrival in Sudata," replied Corvus, and he teleported away as quickly as he arrived.

This is it, thought Hikari. *This is really it. Everything has led to this.*

We will go to Sudata. We will defeat Corvus. We will avenge Liza and all the others he has hurt.

Corvus, I hope you're ready. We're coming.

All of your experimental powers and anything else you throw at us will be no match for us. We have the power of God on our side.

Beat that, Corvus.

Chapter 12

Not too far away from Musura, a young girl was fighting her way through the wilderness. The plants surrounding her were thick and numerous, but they were no match for her tenacity.

"Nothing can stop me!" yelled the girl, as she struggled her way through unknown territory.

In her mind, she was the greatest explorer ever.

She crawled on her knees, not caring if her clothes got dirty. She didn't have a particular objective, and there wasn't a specific place she wanted to get to. She enjoyed the feeling of being in the wilderness, exploring the unknown.

The girl's adventure was abruptly brought to a close when a voice called out to her through the plants.

"Kan!" yelled the voice. It was the voice of a middle aged woman. An irritated middle aged woman.

"Kan!" she repeated. "Where are you?"

The woman spotted her rambunctious daughter crawling through the bushes outside their house and she sighed.

Kan was her five year old daughter. Since the time of her first steps, Kan had always wanted to be an explorer and her mother wasn't sure where she got her aspiration from. Both of her parents were farmers and Kan had never even left the village of Sudata, where she lived with her parents.

Her mother was sure of one thing though. Crawling through bushes and ruining countless sets of clothes was not the kind of exploration she wanted to encourage.

She marched over to her daughter.

"Kan!" she yelled, for the third time. "Get out of there!"

Kan peered through the branches and leaves of the bush and saw her mother's angry face.

"But I'm exploring!" Kan protested.

"You've explored that bush about twenty times," Kan's mother said, losing her temper. "We need you to help with the farm. Come on!"

Kan grudgingly crawled out of the bush. Her short blonde hair was covered in twigs and leaves, and several holes had been torn in her shirt.

"Look at you!" scolded her mother, as she started to brush the dirt off Kan's clothes. "I sewed that shirt last week, and you've already ruined it!"

Kan's mother half dragged Kan to Sudata's small farm. Her father and a few other people from the village were busy at working the land. There were crops that needed to be harvested and all available hands were needed. Kan whinged and dug at the ground with a spade nearly taller than her. She turned to her father.

"Dad, can't you explain to mum that explorers aren't supposed to dig potatoes?" she asked, earnestly.

Her dad laughed. He was far more patient with Kan and her unusual hobby than his wife was.

"Even explorers need to eat," he said.

"Explorers eat leaves," said Kan, sulking.

"If explorers eat leaves, why don't you go and eat some then?" asked her father, amused.

Kan didn't want to eat leaves. She continued to dig with a scowl on her face. They took a break around midday to eat the food Kan's mother had prepared.

While the other villagers were eating and talking, Kan quietly snuck away. She had attempted to get out of the village many, many times, but every attempt had failed miserably. She was confident she would actually be able to get out this time. She reached the path that led out of Sudata, where she saw six strange people walking towards the village.

He parents had always warned her about strangers, but Kan didn't think these people looked scary or dangerous. They were just a little... weird.

Leading the way was a tall girl with a massive pack on her back. Beside her walked another girl, who was talking to her. Four more people brought up the rear, each carrying some sort of weapon.

"Hello!" Kan called out to them.

Rhianna stopped and looked for who called.

"Down here!" said Kan, annoyed she was so small.

"Oh, hello!" said Rhianna when she looked down and saw the young girl standing there. "Is this Sudata?"

"Yes," said Kan, "But it's really, really boring here. All we ever do is eat potatoes."

"Hey, potatoes are good," said Hikari, laughing.

"They're boring!" Kan protested, stamping her foot.

"Don't worry, I think potatoes are boring too," said Kerry, smiling. "These people here don't understand."

"They're not special enough to understand," agreed Kan.

Kerry laughed.

"That's very true," she said. "What's your name?"

"Kan, spelt K –A – N, with a big K and little A and N," she rhymed off proudly.

"Someone knows how to spell!" said Rhianna. "Kan, would you mind taking us to whoever is in charge around here? We have important stuff to tell them."

Kan nodded and she ran off into the village with everyone following behind her.

"Kan!" yelled Kan's mother when Kan returned to the potato field. "Don't run off! You scared us all!"

"Look, mum!" shouted Kan, and she pointed at the six people she had found. "These people want to see the elder!"

The village elder of Sudata was an old man named Molinson. Kan liked him because he gave her sugar canes every time she saw him, much to her mother's dismay.

All the villagers looked at the travellers, curious as to what brought them to Sudata. Sudata wasn't exactly a tourist spot. Visitors were so rare they didn't even have an inn.

"I'm Rhianna, and this is Hikari, Kerry, Noi, Kyros and Saya," Rhianna said politely, as she pointed to everyone in turn. "We're pleased to make your acquaintance."

"They're really nice!" said Kan happily. "Especially the purple haired girl, she thinks potatoes are weird."

Kan's father shook each of the travellers' hands.

"Welcome to Sudata," he said. "I'll bring you to see Elder Molinson."

Elder Molinson lived in a house on the edge of the village. He would normally go out and harvest potatoes, but he thought he was getting too old for farm work. This saddened him, because he liked farming. He had grown up in a large city, and when he was eighteen he left home and set up a farm a few miles away from his home. He named his farm Sudata.

Over the years several people had moved from the city to Sudata because they preferred the tranquillity of the small farming village. Kan was the first person to have lived in Sudata her entire life.

Kan's father led everyone to Molinson's house, and he knocked on the door.

"Come in!" came a cheerful voice from inside the house.

They went in, and saw Elder Molinson sitting in an armchair, reading a book. He had fine white hair and his smiling face was covered in wrinkles.

The house was small and simple; much like the house Hikari grew up in. There was a wooden bed with a straw mattress on top of it and a wood-burning stove in the centre of the room. A large chest lay in the corner of the room, with what looked like horses carved into it. The armchair was positioned next to the stove.

"Who are you fine young people?" he asked.

"They're travellers," replied Kan's father. "They specifically asked to see you."

"Oh! It must be a serious matter then. Pray tell, what have you come all this way to tell me about?"

"Have you heard of the Kelluas?" asked Rhianna, who figured she should find out how much Molinson already knew before she started to explain everything.

Molinson nodded.

"News of them has spread to even this tiny village," he said, solemnly. "It's one of the reasons why we don't want to let little Kan leave the village."

"All the Kelluas have been eliminated except one," explained Rhianna, "and I'm afraid the remaining Kellua is planning to attack Sudata next."

Molinson looked horrified as he sat up in his chair.

"What? No! We need to warn everyone!" he shouted, concerned.

"It's us he's really after," said Rhianna. "If you can get the villagers to a safe hiding place, we will fight him."

"I can't let you fight an enemy as powerful as a Kellua!" protested Molinson.

"Don't worry," said Kerry, and she pointed to the sword attached to her belt, "we're all armed and experienced in battle. We also outnumber him. It should be an easy fight."

Truthfully, Kerry didn't think the fight would be easy. She knew Kan was most at risk. Kerry was all too aware Corvus still needed a child's soul if he wanted to become invincible. Kan was almost certainly his next target. Kerry refused to let Corvus kill any more people. The others all felt the same way.

Molinson nodded.

"Very well then. I will start the evacuation straight away," said Molinson. "The sooner, the better."

"We'll help you with the evacuation," Saya offered.

They left the house. Several people had gathered outside Molinson's house to see what was going on.

"Everyone! I have extremely important news brought to me by these kind travellers!" shouted Molinson.

"We must vacate our village immediately, and we need to seek temporary refuge in Musura!" he explained. "A Kellua is coming to attack this very village!"

The crowd erupted into panicked commotion.

"What's a kellthingymabobber?" asked Kan.

"Something dangerous," said her mother. "We need to get you away from here."

"But danger is exciting for explorers!" she said. Kan looked at Kerry for help.

"I'm afraid your mother is right, Kan," said Kerry. "I know explorers like to be brave, but there is a point where bravery becomes recklessness. Do you know what that word means?"

Kan shook her head.

"It means you put yourself in too much danger, and bad things can happen," Kerry explained. "You can be a brave explorer later. Now, you must go with your parents and the rest of your village. Aren't you excited? You'll get to see a brand new town!"

Kan thought about what Kerry said. She was going to reply, but she was interrupted by a deep voice.

"Words of wisdom indeed, Kerry," said an all too familiar voice.

Hikari looked towards where the voice was coming from.

Perched on top of the roof of Molinson's house was a figure with jet black hair and a cloak of the same colour. He smiled down at Hikari and everyone else.

"Corvus!" yelled Kyros, his voice full of spite.

Corvus threw off his cloak, revealing a layer of battle armour underneath. He had been preparing for this confrontation for some time. While he sent the other Kelluas out on missions he had concentrated on refining his teleportation skills and combat ability. He was confident he could win, even without his comrades.

He turned to Molinson, who was hastily moving the villagers away.

"Not so fast, old man," said Corvus. "There's one thing I want, and then I'll let you all go."

Corvus grinned and teleported from the roof of Molinson's house. He reappeared directly behind where Kan was standing, and he grabbed her.

"You're coming with me!" he yelled.

"Kan!" cried Kerry as she ran towards Corvus. "You challenged us! Fight us now!"

Corvus shook his head, still grinning.

Corvus used his right arm to restrain Kan, who was desperately struggling. He raised his free arm into the air, and it started to glow with a black light.

"Now it's time to play your part, child!" he yelled.

"Let go of her!" cried Kerry, and she tried to pull Kan away from his grasp. Corvus was much stronger than her and he pulled Kan away from the safety of Kerry's arms. Kerry and the others watched in horror as Corvus started the process of soul extraction. There were no bright lights or any other obvious displays of power, but Kan slowly stopped struggling and became more and more lifeless. Kan's mother and the other villagers looked on in horror.

"Everyone! If we all attack at once, we should be able to free her!" Kerry shouted.

Everyone drew their weapons and charged towards Corvus at the same time. They were unable to hit the back of his head, which was protected by his armour, so the attack wasn't fatal. It was, however, strong enough to make him relinquish his grip on Kan's arm.

Kan fell to the ground.

Kerry ran over to her and shook her, but Kan did not respond. Her eyes were open and she was still breathing, but Corvus had left her in a vegetative state. Kerry stood by her, determined not to let Corvus touch the child again.

Corvus snarled as he staggered back several steps.

"You meddlesome maggots," he growled. "Just a moment longer and I would have completed the experiment!"

The others charged, desperate to attack Corvus again before he could recover.

This is it, thought Hikari. *It all comes down to this. All we have been fighting for. I can finally avenge Liza.*

God, give us strength.

They all attacked Corvus at once. But before they could connect, he floated off the ground and hurled black orbs of energy at them. Hikari dodged all the orbs thrown in her direction, and continued to relentlessly attack him.

Corvus made the most of his abilities by making sure he remained in a floating position. He also used teleportation to his advantage, escaping from harm's way every time any of the humans got close enough to attack him. Hikari's rage increased each time she went to attack but ended up bringing her scythe down on nothing but air.

"You're going down!" screamed Saya, and they continued to fight.

Saya and Kyros ran towards Corvus with great speed and brought their weapons down on the armour protecting the back of his head before he had a chance to escape. With a synchronised and graceful motion, they shattered his head protection. The broken fragments fell to the ground like shards of glass.

Meanwhile, Kerry stood protectively over Kan and relentlessly counterattacked Corvus each time he came near her to finish what he had started.

Corvus fired an orb towards Hikari. She wasn't able to dodge it quickly enough, and it struck her leg. She cried out over the immense pain of seared flesh but was determined to keep fighting for Liza's sake. The long battle took its toll on everyone. Corvus wasn't shooting with the same velocity he had been before, and Hikari and the others were ready to drop their weapons and give up. But there was one thing that kept each of them going.

For Noi, he kept going because he didn't want to let his friends down. Especially Kerry.

Rhianna fought to please her parents, and to save her kingdom from Corvus.

Kerry fought with her timid friend Kamitika in mind. The castle librarian had had the courage to stand up to two Kelluas so surely she could muster the strength to dispatch one, right?

Saya fought for her mother, and for Grace.

Kyros fought for the other two Kelluas who had already died as a result of Corvus and his schemes.

Hikari fought with a picture of Liza smiling in her head.

However, they all had a common source of inspiration. They fought for their Saviour, Jesus Christ. It was in Him and through Him they drew the strength necessary to continue.

"Father God, give us the strength to claim victory in the name of Jesus!" Hikari cried out.

"Jesus? Please, child! Your God's not even real!" Corvus spat. "He cannot help you!"

"We'll see about that!" Hikari retaliated. "If our God is for us, who can be against us? You're going down Corvus!"

Sustained by the Holy Spirit, they were able to continue fighting with renewed energy and strength. On their own they were nothing more than a group of kids and two former outcasts. But with God's help, nothing seemed impossible.

Exhausted and no longer possessing even the strength to teleport, Corvus allowed more openings to attack him. They dealt many debilitating blows, but their main target remained every Kellua's primary weakness: the back of the head.

Corvus made a desperate attempt to launch another offensive assault but Hikari countered, slamming her scythe down on the back of his head.

Corvus collapsed. His body slumped to the ground in defeat.

They should have been overjoyed with their victory but they were too concerned for Kan to celebrate.

She was still alive, but they didn't know if she'd ever regain her soul. Would she stay limp and lifeless forever? Hikari couldn't let that happen.

They were in need of one more miracle before their quest was complete.

"Kan!" cried Kan's mother, and she ran to her daughter who was lying in Kerry's arms.

Kan was brought into her house and laid down on her bed. The villager with the most advanced medical knowledge examined her. To his amazement, it seemed as if there was nothing wrong. Her heart was beating, she was breathing and there were no signs of injury. However, she was nonresponsive to everything they tried.

"How do you recover a soul?" Rhianna asked quietly, watching the doctor's helpless despair as he examined Kan.

"I don't know if that's even possible," replied Kerry, with tears welling in her eyes.

Hikari looked at Kan, who was as blank as ever.

How to recover a soul. She thought. *How…*

Hikari felt the battle against the Kelluas wouldn't truly be a victory unless Kan recovered. She refused to let another child lose their life. It was like watching Liza die all over again.

It felt like a hollow victory.

Kan lay motionless in bed with her family and some other villagers surrounding her. Kan's mother was being comforted by her husband as she dried her tears with a handkerchief. The scene broke Hikari's heart. Kerry turned to Hikari, her eyes lit up with excitement.

"Hikari, what did you do when I was hit by an avalanche? What did we do before fighting Corvus?" she said earnestly. "We prayed! Listen up everyone. There is power in prayer. If God is willing to heal her, He might grant us the power of the Holy Spirit at our fingertips."

"Yes!" Hikari cried, suddenly understanding Kerry's excitement. She turned to face everyone. "All of you! Do you really want to save Kan?"

There was a unanimous agreement. Rhianna pulled Hikari over.

"Musura isn't a Christian town, you know," Rhianna whispered. "If all these people originated from there none of them will believe you."

"If they're not believers now, perhaps they will be after they see God's power for themselves," Hikari replied with confidence. "Just like Kerry when woke up unharmed after the avalanche, I believe it is God's will to save Kan. If we all join together and pray then hopefully God will decide to let Kan live!"

"Let's do this!" Kerry agreed enthusiastically.

Inspired by Kerry and Hikari's confidence, Rhianna turned to face the villagers as if she was about to make a royal address to the people.

"Villagers of Sudata, if I can have your attention please. We need your help if we are to heal little Kan. I don't know if any of you are familiar with Christianity," she said. "You have probably heard the legends but I know the idea of some all-loving god may seem ridiculous to some of you. After all, we live in a fallen world and there's constant suffering all around us. I was raised to believe in a God who loved and cared for me, but I let logic rule my heart and I decided He couldn't possibly exist. However, thanks to my sister's influence, I now see there is so much more in this world than logic can ever hope to grasp."

"Princess Rhianna speaks the truth," Hikari said. "I know things may appear hopeless for little Kan right now. But we believe in a God who raised his Son, Jesus Christ, from death so our souls could be saved. Little Kan may be alive but her soul is in jeopardy. I'm asking you to cast aside your doubts and put your faith in Jesus. We believe He does all things for the good of those who love Him. And we believe He has the power to heal little Kan and to restore her soul. If we all join hands and pray for Kan's safety I'm certain God will hear us and answer our request for help! God can perform miracles in even the direst of circumstances."

There was a rumble of commotion among the villagers.

"Okay, we'll do it," declared Molinson, who was standing in the doorway. No-one had noticed him come in. "Anything for Kan."

The villagers had absolute trust in Molinson, so soon everybody in the room had joined hands. It was Kan's mother who spoke next.

"Please God, if you are there!" she cried desperately. "Please save my daughter! She's too young to be taken away from me!"

The noise in the room erupted as every person in the room began begging for Kan's safety. Some fell to their knees.

At first there was no response from Kan. Everyone in the room was holding their breath, unable to bear the suspense. Then, after what felt like an eternity, the little girl abruptly opened her eyes and sat up, looking extremely confused.

"Kan!" exclaimed her mother before scooping her daughter into her arms and hugging her tight.

Kan started crying in her mother's arms.

"Mummy, the scary man was mean to me," she said between sobs.

"You're safe now, I promise."

An applause broke out amongst the villagers. Hikari was overcome with joy.

Finally, her quest was complete. She'd defeated Corvus, made new lifelong friends and had come to know Jesus Christ as her Lord and Saviour.

Liza was avenged.

Chapter 13

It's over.

Hikari sat on the grass on the outskirts of Sudata, looking back at the small farming village. It had been five days since defeating Corvus, and they had spent that time teaching the villagers about their faith. The weather was mild and a gentle breeze was blowing through the air. The grass was emerald green and was dotted with daisies. It was extremely peaceful.

The group had spent the past week in Sudata being treated like heroes. Kan had made a full recovery and was back to crawling around in bushes. Her mother was a bit softer with her, but was still dismayed at the amount of holes she tore in her clothes.

Everything's in place. The Kelluas are all gone. Liza has been avenged.

The quest had not taken that long, but to Hikari it felt like a lifetime since she was in Honif complaining about broccoli. The fact her journey had finally come to an end was still sinking in.

What will I do now?

"You look awfully serious, Snappytaps."

Hikari almost jumped out of her skin when she turned around and saw Kerry standing there.

"When did you get here?" Hikari exclaimed.

"You were so deep in thought a herd of monsters travelling your way probably wouldn't have fazed you," Kerry said matter-of-factly.

Kerry lay down in the grass beside Hikari.

"Isn't this nice, Snappytaps? Finally, we can relax," she said as she spread her arms out dramatically on the grass. "And the villagers all treat us like we're awesome! I almost don't want to return to the castle after all this hero treatment…"

"So you're returning to Alana?" Hikari asked.

She sighed. Hikari knew her friends could not stay in Sudata forever. She was just shocked at how suddenly they were leaving. Kyros and Saya had already decided they were going to go to Noi's hometown of Alburn and see if they could get work from Noi's old master, the potter. They would finally be able to live a normal life with humans. Of course, Hikari was happy for them, but the thought of parting ways was almost too painful to bear.

"I could live here forever, but Rhianna needs to go back. She is next in line to the throne, after all…" Kerry moaned. "I promised Rhianna I'd go back with her. I'm going to try and strike some deal with my parents so I don't have to study as hard."

Hikari looked at the ground and fiddled with a blade of grass.

"I don't know what I'm going to do," she confessed. "I might end up tagging along with Kyros and Saya, as crazy as that sounds."

"You know, the minister at the castle is always looking for people to teach. Maybe you could see if he's willing to take you on as an apprentice of sorts? He'll teach you all about the Bible," Kerry suggested happily. "Then you can live with Rhianna, Kamitika and me! You can smuggle me out of the castle during my tutoring sessions!"

"Do you really think that's a possibility?" Hikari asked, awestruck.

"Yeah!" replied Kerry, jumping up. "You could definitely study at the castle!"

The idea filled Hikari with so much happiness. She would be able to live with her friends and study a religion she was desperate to know more about. Even still, a thread of doubt tugged at her. Would they really accept her? A commoner from the island?

"Let's talk to Rhianna!" Kerry declared, before grabbing Hikari by the arm and hauling her off the ground.

They ran back to the village to find Rhianna, excited about their plan. They went to the house where they had been staying. When they found her she was repacking her and Kerry's bags.

"Oh, Kerry!" she looked up and smiled. "I was going through your bag and I was wondering if you could leave some of your stuff here? You bought an unbelievable amount of socks at the Musura festival..."

"I need every single one of those socks!" Kerry protested. "They all hold great memories. I'll be able to look at them and say 'Hey, I was wearing those socks the day we defeated Corvus!' They're personal treasures!"

Rhianna sighed and tried to shove the socks into what little space was left in the bag.

"Anyway, that's not what I came for!" Kerry said excitedly. "I came to discuss Hikari's future!"

"Ah, that's right," Rhianna said, setting the bag down. "I meant to ask you what you were planning on doing."

"At first I considered staying here, but I would be lonely without any of you. I also thought I might join Kyros and Saya to find work in Alburn, but with them being so close now I didn't want to feel like a third wheel," Hikari explained. "Then Kerry suggested I speak to the minister at Alana and see if he can teach me."

"You'd like to stay in the castle?" Rhianna asked, surprised.

"Don't you think it would be awesome?" Kerry exclaimed. "She could become one of these super-smart scholar people. You'd be queen, Hikari would be an apprentice and I'd be... court jester."

"We have no court jester," Rhianna said sarcastically. "But it does sound like a good idea for Hikari to come back with us. As future monarch, I think she'd be a fine addition to the court."

"Thank you!" Hikari exclaimed and she hugged Rhianna.

Finally, I have found a new home.

***

The next morning, the group prepared to leave Sudata to begin their last journey together. They would part ways in Alburn. Noi was also planning on returning to Alburn to seek work along with Kyros and Saya, with hopes he would be able to find a trade that suited him more than pottery.

The people of Sudata gave the group many gifts to thank them for everything they had done for the village.

"Please don't leave!" Kan cried as she clung to Kerry's leg. "It's boring when you're not here!"

"I think your poor mother has had enough stress to last a lifetime," Kerry laughed. "Being boring is not as bad as you'd think. You're lucky, I have to go and study Latin now!"

"As if you're actually going to study," Rhianna muttered to herself.

Rhianna patted Kan's head.

"If you are a good girl now, when you're older you can be an explorer. There's a whole land mass to the east no-one has even charted yet. It looks terrible on my maps, so one day when I am Queen I want you to help me fill in that region."

Kan's eyes lit up.

"Yes!" she shouted. "I'll do that someday!"

Now Corvus was gone, Kan and her family would be able to live in peace once more. Seeing Kan's smiling face was worth more than any gift the villagers had given Hikari. Molinson, Kan and all the other people of Sudata waved as the group set off on the path towards their new lives.

Compared to the trials they had faced, the days of walking to Alburn were a breeze. They took down any attacking monsters with ease. Even so, the fact every step they took brought them closer to their day of parting hung heavily in the air until at last, the familiar city of Alburn came into view.

Well, there it is. My home, Noi thought sadly. *The idea of going back to work now is hard. After the excitement of the last few days I really can't imagine it all ending like this.*

Kerry noticed how down Noi looked. She too felt sad at the thought of leaving Noi. She would have no-one to tease anymore.

"We'll come and visit lots," Kerry promised, keeping everyone's spirits up.

When they reached the city Kyros and Saya went to the potter to see if he would hire them, while the others went to the inn which was now reopened. It was evening, so they postponed goodbyes until the morning. Noi also decided to go and do a bit of job hunting before the day was out.

Kerry watched him exit the inn and the heavy feeling that pulled at her heart intensified. Without telling the others where she was going she ran out of the inn.

"Wait! Hang on a second!" she called towards Noi's retreating figure.

The streets were bathed in the faint light of dusk. Everyone had already returned home, so Kerry and Noi were the only ones left standing in the street. Noi turned around.

"Oh hi, Kerry," he smiled. "Did I leave something? Or did you think of another insult you wanted to send my way?"

"No...umm..." Kerry stammered as she wondered what she should say.

"Do you want to help me look for work?" he asked, raising his eyebrows in curiosity.

"No way!" Kerry said. "There's no way you're going to go into another apprenticeship you won't enjoy!"

"I don't have a lot of choice," Noi said with a chuckle and a sad smile. "I have no idea what I really want to do with my life but I'm not royalty like you. My options are kind of limited, Kerry."

"Let's fix that," Kerry said quietly. "If you leave now I'll have no-one to make fun of, and you'll have to slave away working for the rest of your life doing something you probably won't even enjoy..."

Kerry took a deep breath and raised her voice.

"Noi, I suppose what I want to say is... well... I want you to marry me, Noi! I want you to be my prince!"

Noi was stunned into silence. For several seconds, they both stood still without saying anything.

Although their backgrounds were as different as could be, both of them had always struggled with feeling accepted. For both Kerry and Noi, their journey together had meant much more than defeating Corvus. It had been the first time in their lives they had felt truly accepted. And even though they were both hesitant to admit it, it was the first time they had felt another unfamiliar emotion.

Noi suddenly ran towards Kerry and embraced her.

"Yes," he whispered into her ear as he lifted her up off the ground. "I'm in love with you, Kerry. I had no idea you felt the same about me."

Kerry began to tear up.

"Don't think I'm only saying this because I don't want find a job," Noi said with a laugh. "I actually wanted to confess my feelings to you before, but I was worried it was too sudden. And I didn't think you would love me back. I've never really been in love with a girl before, but I know I really feel happy when I'm with you, Kerry. And I can't imagine life without you."

"Oh Noi, it makes me so happy to hear you say that. I'm in love with you too!!" Kerry exclaimed before crying tears of joy in Noi's arms.

I thought I'd never find true love. My parents always tried to find a husband for Rhianna, because she needed to have children to continue the royal line. I was left to the side.

Now I realize how blessed I am. I have a gift poor Rhianna will probably never experience.

I've been able to choose who I love.

***

Finally, the dreaded day of parting came. Kyros and Saya were able to get an apprenticeship with Noi's old master, and they were going to live in his house. As it turned out, Kelluas were surprisingly gifted with the raw skills necessary to master the art of pottery. The fellowship of friends all stood at the exit of Alburn together.

"I'm sorry, Hikari," Kyros said. "I'm so sorry about what I did. I'm sorry about Liza."

Hikari shook her head.

"I forgave you a long time ago, Kyros. You were as much a victim of Corvus as my sister was."

"Forgive me too," Saya begged. "I feel terrible about everything I've done."

"Come on!" Kerry said. "Let's stop dwelling in the past. We've all forgiven you. You're our friends now, and will be for life."

Saya smiled.

"We can't ever repay your kindness," she said, getting misty eyed.

"Don't cry or I'll cry too!" Rhianna pleaded.

Kyros and Saya embraced everyone in turn. They were all crying, even Noi and Kyros.

"You can come to the castle anytime!" Rhianna assured.

"Come on Saya, let's go," Kyros said gently. "We have work to do."

"Good luck with that old man..." Noi said, remembering his master.

"Goodbye!" Kyros and Saya said in unison, and they turned around and walked towards the potter's house.

Rhianna wiped her eyes.

"Are we going to have to do another emotional goodbye now?" she asked Noi. "I've never cried so much in my life."

"We'll miss you a lot," Hikari said to Noi.

"Actually..." Noi began.

"What my fiancé is trying to say is we're going to get married!" Kerry proudly announced with enthusiasm.

"WHAT?" Rhianna and Hikari exclaimed in unison.

"My little sister is engaged to be married? At your age?" Rhianna said in a flustered tone. "Well, I suppose if it's Noi you're marrying then that's ok with me."

Hikari smiled.

"I always thought you'd make a good couple," she said.

Noi took Kerry's hand and she blushed.

"I'm going to look after Kerry for the rest of my life," he announced.

I've never been so happy, Hikari thought. *Kerry and Rhianna used to hate each other. Now they've become closer than ever. Noi and Kerry have fallen in love. Even Saya and Kyros can now live normal, peaceful lives.*

Comforted by the soothing spirit of fellowship, the four friends began their journey towards their new lives together.

***

Later that night, Hikari dreamt of Liza. However, this dream felt far more real than any of the other dreams that had plagued her sleep before. Hikari was standing in an infinite field of whiteness. There was nothing in the space except a soft glowing light which surrounded her from all angles. Hikari was overcome with a feeling of peace and tranquillity.

From the source of the light, a figure emerged. It was Liza. She still had her childish figure, but she looked far more mature than Hikari had ever seen her. The light surrounded her, as if it was protecting her from any harm.

"I love you, Hikari. You've made me really happy by finding your way in the world again by embracing the love of Jesus," Liza said to Hikari.

Her voice was different; it was not that of a normal six year old. If Hikari had to describe it in one word, it would be angelic.

"I was always happy to be your sister when we shared life together. When I died and came to this place, I watched over you, cheering you on each and every step of the way."

Hikari tried to speak, but she couldn't. She was too overcome with emotion to say anything.

"As I was dying, I feared you wouldn't be able to live on your own," Liza continued. "But then I watched you meet loads of friends. I was really happy for you, especially for accepting Jesus into your heart. We are so proud of you Hikari!"

We? thought Hikari, confused.

"Yes Hikari, we are so proud of you," said a new voice.

Hikari gasped as she recognised the figure of her deceased father materialising next to Liza. His torn work clothes and scruffy facial hair were gone. Just like Liza, he was clothed in the light. He looked like nothing of this world but she recognized him all the same.

"Satan tried to use Corvus as an instrument of hate to destroy others but you overcame him through your love for your friends, your family, and your Saviour," her father said with a smile.

"Your father is right, Hikari. We are so proud of you, my precious daughter!" chimed a soft feminine voice. It was Hikari's mother.

The kind, motherly look in her eyes was still there, as Hikari remembered it.

Hikari began to weep without restraint.

"Mum! Dad! Liza! I want to stay here with you!" she cried. "I don't want you to leave me again!"

"You're time has not yet come," explained the kind voice of her mother. "You still have work to do on Maysea, Hikari. Jesus will be with you as you obey his command to go forth and make disciples of all nations. And we will be watching, cheering, and waiting for you to come home to us."

"Don't worry. It won't be long now. We'll be together again soon, Hikari," Liza said. "I love you."

Hikari embraced her sister one last time as her dream came to an end.

"And God shall wipe away all tears from their eyes; and there shall be no more death, neither sorrow, nor crying, neither shall there be any more pain: for the former things are passed away." - Revelation 21:4

About Erin Burnett

Having enjoyed writing from a young age Erin Burnett felt compelled to write for Christ, and wrote the first semi-readable draft of *Liza's Avenger* on a school computer when she was thirteen. Since then she has joined Belfast Writers' Group and strives to improve her writing. She firmly believes that with God, nothing is impossible.

In addition to writing Erin enjoys cycling and travelling. Of the 58 countries she has visited, her favourite is Japan. She is currently a sixth form student and lives with her wonderfully supportive family in Belfast, Northern Ireland. She aspires to study theology at university level.

https://www.facebook.com/lizasavenger

42150175R00115